THE GREAT MOSHLING EGG

PUFFIN BOOKS

Published by the Penguin Group
Penguin Books Ltd, 80 Strand, London WC2R 0RL, England
Penguin Group (USA) Inc., 375 Hudson Street, New York, New York 10014, USA
Penguin Group (Canada), 90 Eglinton Avenue East, Suite 700, Toronto, Ontario, Canada M4P 2Y3
Penguin Ireland, 25 St Stephen's Green, Dublin 2, Ireland
Penguin Group (Australia), 707 Collins Street, Melbourne, Victoria 3008, Australia
Penguin Books India Pvt Ltd, 11 Community Centre, Panchsheel Park, New Delhi – 110 017, India
Penguin Group (NZ), 67 Apollo Drive, Rosedale, Auckland 0632, New Zealand
Penguin Books (South Africa) (Pty) Ltd, Block D, Rosebank Office Park, 181 Jan Smuts Avenue,
Parktown North, Gauteng 2193, South Africa

Penguin Books Ltd, Registered Offices: 80 Strand, London WC2R 0RL, England

puffinbooks.com

First published 2013
002

Text and illustrations copyright © Mind Candy Ltd, 2013
Moshi Monsters is a trademark of Mind Candy Ltd. All rights reserved.
The moral right of the author and illustrator has been asserted.

Set in Adobe Garamond Pro
Printed in Great Britain by Clays Ltd, St Ives plc

British Library Cataloguing in Publication Data
A CIP catalogue record for this book is available from the British Library

ISBN: 978-1-401-35069-1

FSC
MIX
Paper from
responsible sources
FSC™ C018179

THE GREAT MOSHLING EGG

Jonathan Green

Based on a screenplay by
Steve Cleverley and Jocelyn Stevenson

PUFFIN

CONTENTS

CHAPTER ONE

Somewhere, Deep
in the Jungle . . .

It was another swelteringly hot day deep in the jungle, but then every day in the jungle was swelteringly hot. Insects buzzed and chirruped while strange hooting cries echoed above the forest canopy. Eyes peered from the darkness beneath the trees watching the progress of the strange party. Led by Buster Bumblechops – the world's premier Moshling collector – a host of porters trudged through the jungle, glancing anxiously about them at every strange sound they heard.

Buster pushed aside another dangling palm

frond and halted. Rising out of the jungle before him were the tumbled ruins of an ancient temple. At the top of a flight of steps, an opening yawned in the rock. Beyond, the explorers could see nothing but darkness.

Buster tensed and took a deep breath. The object of his quest lay within reach at last. This was the place, he was sure of it.

'This way,' the Moshlingologist mumbled as he climbed the steps to the entrance. 'No one's been here for centuries!'

Buster stopped, realizing he was alone. The nervous porters were huddled together at the bottom of the steps, peering up at him nervously.

'Keep up!' he called to them before setting off into the darkness, a flaming torch held high in his hand.

A writhing mass of creepy-crawlies appeared as his torch cast its flickering light over the walls and floor, before scuttling away into dark recesses and cracks in the floor. But that wasn't all that was disturbed by his arrival. Squeaking, a host of bats dropped from the roof of the tunnel. Startled by the noise and the buffeting of the bats' wings as they flew past, he ran. He didn't stop running until he was deep inside the temple.

Strange carvings covered the crumbling walls. Exhausted after his flight through the darkness, Buster paused to rest, leaning against an ancient stone plinth.

'Phew! What in the name of Snufflepeeps?' he gasped as the stone shifted and began to sink into the ground.

Buster jumped again as, with a deep grating rumble, one of the wall carvings opened, revealing another tunnel.

Without a second's thought, he entered this new passageway.

And there before him, sitting on another carved stone plinth, was a magnificent egg.

'Ahhh!' Buster gasped in amazement. It was the treasure he had been seeking. The ultimate prize was within his reach at last.

Moments later, Buster emerged from the temple ruins, his Moshling porters gathering round, both delighted and surprised to see him alive, and still in one piece.

'At last I've found it!' the Moshling hunter extraordinaire announced, holding his prize aloft for all to see. The Moshlings fell to their knees in wonder, bowing in the presence of the legendary object. 'The Great Moshling Egg!'

As they marvelled at the marvellous egg, the porters began to chant. 'Umba chucka umba chucka umba chucka.'

Buster turned, making sure that everyone had seen the egg, and promptly tripped over a rock.

'Ahhhh!' he cried as he tumbled down a flight of crumbling stone steps. 'Ooof! My leg!'

Buster reached the bottom of the stairs and then found himself sliding down a rocky slop. The precious egg flew from his hands.

'The egg!' he cried in panic. 'Ouch!' he added as he

bumped over the rocks on his backside. 'Ooooh!'

But his eyes were on the egg all the time as it spun through the air. As the egg tumbled towards the ground, Buster leapt forward and snatched it out of the air.

'Ah-ha!'

The Great Moshling Egg was safe – for now!

CHAPTER TWO

Hi Yaa Hurricane!

It was another peaceful morning in Moshi World. The sun was shining as a flutterby landed on a Moshling flower growing in a certain garden not far from Monstro City, where a curious yellow Moshling with flappy green ears and a snuffling snout was munching the grass. Mr. Snoodle was enjoying a mid-morning snack. Unfortunately the morning wasn't going to stay peaceful for long.

'Hey, they picked meeeee!' Katsuma yelled, bursting out of his house in excitement, and tripping over Mr. Snoodle. 'Oooof! Hey, watch where you're doodling, Snoodle!'

Seeing the annoyed expression on Katsuma's face, Mr. Snoodle scurried through a gap in the garden fence, escaping to the peace and quiet of Poppet's backyard next door.

Snoodle sidled up to Poppet who was humming softly as she watered the Moshling seeds she had just planted. She was humming along to the music some Tunie Moshlings – Oompah, Wallop, Plinky and HipHop – were playing nearby.

'Poppet! Poppet!' Katsuma's face appeared over the top of the fence. 'I've got an important announcement!'

'Ooh, stop the music, will you?'

Startled, the Tunies stopped playing.

'I've got an important announcement,' the excited Moshi tried again. 'Roary Scrawl is making a documentary – a movie all about Monstro City!'

'Yes, Katsuma,' said Poppet, who was now giving Mr. Snoodle a cuddle. 'And?'

'And he chose me to be the star!'

Poppet picked up her watering can again. 'You mean, you talked him into it.'

Katsuma ignored her. 'Oh boy, I can't wait to show him my brand new Four Claw Hi Yaa Hurricane!' He thrust a Mash Up trading card detailing the move in her direction.

'Hii-' Katsuma began as he leapt into the air, making a brave attempt at the move, and then, '-yaaaaaaaaowwww!' he finished, yowling in pain, as he got his foot stuck in the fence.

'Er, very impressive,' Poppet remarked as she helped her friend get his foot out of the fence. 'Is that all?' she asked as she returned to her gardening, sprinkling more seeds on the ground before giving them a good soaking with her watering can. 'Because I'm trying to attract ultra-rare Moshlings, and they like music with their flowers.'

She turned to the Tunies.

'Two, three, four!'

The musical Moshlings readied themselves to play.

'Stop!' Katsuma yelled, just as they were about to strike up the band. The Tunies slumped back down.

'Didn't you hear me? I'm going to be a gooperstar! Hi Yaa Hurricane!' he yelled, as he attempted his crazy kung fu move again.

A carelessly abandoned garden rake lay on the ground nearby. A thumpkin lay beside it.

At his second attempt, Katsuma executed his Hi Yaa Hurricane move perfectly. Poppet and Snoodle looked on admiringly.

He landed on the ground, just missing the rake as he did so, his face lighting up in delight.

'Hey, Poppet,' – he took a step forward – 'did you see my mo-' and stepped on the rake.

The handle shot up, launching the thumpkin into the air, and whacked him in the face. Stunned, Katsuma stumbled backwards and fell into a wheelbarrow as the thumpkin came back down to earth, and landed on his head.

'Come on,' Poppet chuckled, unable to help herself, 'let's go find Roary.'

Nothing was going to dent Katsuma's enthusiasm.

Shaking off the thumpkin, he leapt out of the wheelbarrow.

'Yeah! I've got an appointment with gooperstardom! Hit it, Moshlings!'

Delighted at being permitted to play again, Oompah, Wallop, Plinky and HipHop began to parp, bang, tinkle and beatbox for all they were worth.

But as the friends set off for Monstro City, none of them saw a shadowy figure pluck Plinky from his place in the band and scarper faster than Blingo could rap.

CHAPTER THREE

Main Street Madness

Leaving Katsuma's garden, the flutterby flittered after the friends. The Main Street of Monstro City lay below, filled with monsters and their Moshlings going about their business. Like Bubba the Bouncer and Fifi the Oochie Poochie he was taking for a walk.

But one Moshling in particular stood out as he flounced down the street. It was Flumpy the Pluff, only it wasn't Flumpy-like at all. Pluffs are normally cheerful, carefree and friendly, but as he stumbled along Main Street, Flumpy kept bumping into passers-by. He even managed to kick over a seed cart. As the seeds rolled across the ground, Moshis went flying as their feet shot out from under them.

With the street descending into chaos, Flumpy grabbed a canister of throat spray from a street vendor – without paying for it! – and while Bubba was distracted, he stole Fifi away from him, lead and all!

By the time Bubba noticed Flumpy and Fifi were half way down the road, the Pluff, who looked like a big, white ball of fur on legs, was giggling to himself. Meanwhile, the distraught bouncer collapsed and burst into tears – more Blubber than Bubba now.

Flumpy sidled past a gang of Moshis talking with Roary Scrawl in the street, and when he was sure no one was looking, flipped open a manhole cover. He quickly kicked the quivering Fifi into the hole before jumping in after the pooch, as the manhole cover rattled back into place.

As Flumpy did his vanishing act, approaching

from the other end of the street, Katsuma and Poppet headed for the diner.

The diner was bustling with monsters by the time Katsuma and Poppet arrived with Mr. Snoodle in tow. In fact the place was packed with monsters and Moshlings of all descriptions. In the centre of the throng stood Roary Scrawl, the multi-eyed editor of *The Daily Growl*. The TV was on, but everyone present was ignoring it and hanging on Roary's every word instead.

'Yeah, I've always wanted to make a documentary about Monstro City,' Roary was explaining. 'I mean editing *The Daily Growl* is a great gig, but making movies?! Now you're squawking!'

Everyone nodded in agreement at the editor's words of wisdom, including the weird-looking Moshling that was little more than one huge mechanical eye, twiddly aerial and swivelling side jets, hovering close to Roary's shoulder. It was Blinki the All-Seeing Moment Muncher.

Seizing his chance and leaving his friends behind, Katsuma rushed over to introduce himself.

'Mr Scrawl, allow me to introduce myself,' the over-excited monster began, demonstrating his trademark kung fu move he'd been practising all morning. 'Katsuma, the star of your movie! Hi Yaa Hurricane!'

But before he could go for the big finish, Blinki flew in, stopping him in his tracks.

'Uh . . . Yeah. Have you met Blinki?' Roary said. 'He's my Moshling-cam partner in movie-making magic. Wherever we all go, Blinki here will follow.'

The Moshling-cam nodded eagerly in agreement.

Katsuma remained frozen, mid-move. 'I, but . . . Did you say wherever *we* all go? Don't you mean wherever you go? And by "you", I kinda mean me? I'm the star of this movie!' said Katsuma confidently. But then, suddenly, he wasn't so sure. 'Right?'

'Well, here's the thing,' Roary said, half a dozen of his roving eyes looking in the direction of Poppet, who had now caught up with Katsuma. 'I'm thinking your friend Poppet here has bags of potential too.'

Poppet smiled sweetly, while Katsuma pulled a face like he'd just eaten a whole packet of Barfmallows.

'I've decided that the two of you should star in this movie. A double act! "Monstro City with Poppet and Katsuma".'

Katsuma stared at Roary, his mouth open, his face frozen in horror. 'But . . . '

'So glad you agree!' Roary grinned, 'because I think the rest of your pals should tag along too.'

Katsuma swallowed hard. 'You mean Furi, Luvli, Diavlo and . . . '

A loud burp silenced the entire diner, and Zommer pulled himself out from under a table, still glugging from a Wobble-ade bottle.

'Zommer?' Poppet said, surprised. 'How long have you been here?'

'Yeah, it's OK as long as I don't scratch it or shower,' the monster drawled. Everyone in the diner stared at him, sporting a range of confused expressions on their faces.

Staggering to his feet, Zommer burped again and this time his eye fell out, landing in a glass on the table.

'See? This guy's a natural!' Roary declared, clearly thrilled at the prospect of having the Wobble-ade glugging rocker appear in his movie.

But Katsuma wasn't. 'Look, Mr Scrawl, I like hanging out with my pals, but making a movie is a whole different barrel of Sploshlings!'

'Ahhhhhhhh!' Zommer had stopped drinking and was staring deep into Blinki eye-cam. It was hard to tell how the mechanical eye-bot was feeling, but from where Katsuma was standing, Blinki was looking more freaked out than fascinated. Zommer, on the other hand, appeared hypnotized.

'Sure, sure, but just look at Luvli over there,' Roary went on, pointing to the other side of the eatery where Luvli was giving some of the customers a demonstration of her special brand of magic, food and plates spinning around her head as her magical stalk glowed with mystical power. 'She's one sassy monster!'

Luvli's audience started to applaud. Local fisherman Billy Bob Baitman was so impressed he climbed onto a levitating plate in the hope of giving the heart-shaped monster a kiss.

'All them thar curves and me with no brakes!' he declared making a grab for her. At that precise instant Luvli cancelled her magic, causing Billy Bob to tumble to the ground as the plates came crashing down on his head.

'You see, darlings?' Luvli said, smiling and blowing Billy Bob a kiss, 'when I'm good I'm really good. But when I'm bad, I'm even better!'

BOOM!

As well as interrupting Luvli, the unexpected explosion rattled the windows of the diner, sending every Moshling in the place diving for cover under the tables.

CHAPTER FOUR

Hothead Hoo-HAA

Diavlo's head had just exploded. The hot-headed monster wasn't happy.

'If I've told them once, I've told them a gazillion times,' he fumed staring at the plate of sausages in front of him, getting angrier and angrier with every word he uttered, 'I like my sausages singed, scorched and roasted 'til they're toasted into oblivion!'

Furious now, his face red with rage, Diavlo picked up the plate of sausages and tipped the food into the hole in the top of his head. He tensed, smoke rising from the crater. A moment later, the sausages – now black and shrivelled – popped out again.

Opening wide, Diavlo caught them in his mouth. Squirting a mouthful of ketchup in after them, he swallowed the lot in one great gulp.

'Mmm,' he said, closing his eyes in delight as he savoured the taste of the burnt sausages, several smoke rings of pleasure puffing from the top of his head, 'carbonized!'

'And that Diavlo cracks me up!' Roary laughed, holding his sides as he doubled up.

'Sure, he's a blast,' Katsuma replied, sounding wholly unimpressed, 'but he and the others . . . They're just the fries to my burger. The sprinkles to my sundae. The . . .'

'Pickles to my pancakes!' suggested Furi as he ambled past, his eyes zooming in on the tray of pickles being carried by an Uppity Croc Monsieur waiter, wearing a smart black jacket and a bright red bow tie. The hulking monster wandered off again, now following the tray of food.

'I almost forgot Furi!' Roary gasped, waving in the

other monster's direction. Furi was already tucking into a huge pile of pickly pancakes at a table nearby. 'That big ol' hairball's a scream!'

'Furi?' Katsuma cried in disbelief. 'Next thing you'll be telling me that . . . '

Before he could say anything else, Poppet quickly popped a paw over his mouth so that the unkind comparison he was about to make sounded like nothing more than an incomprehensible muffled mumble.

'It'll be fine, Mr Scrawl,' Poppet said, giving Roary a reassuring smile.

Katsuma continued to try to talk through Poppet's paw. 'No, it won't be fine, I . . . ' Katsuma managed before Poppet could put her other paw over the monster's mouth as well.

It was clear that Roary was fast running out of patience. 'You know we could always get some real talent,' he said. 'This town's full of wannabes.'

Katsuma pulled Poppet's paw free from in front of his mouth, a sour scowl on his face. 'Wannabes? Mr

Scrawl, you are looking at a gonna-be and . . . '

Roary glared at him. Katsuma wilting under the editor's furious stare.

'OK, OK. I've, er, gotta call my agent.' Downbeat and dejected, Katsuma slunk away, his shoulders sagging, his body language saying it all.

'What's with him?' Roary asked.

'He's just being . . . ' Poppet struggled to think of a suitable explanation. 'He's just being . . . Katsuma.'

CHAPTER FIVE

We Interrupt this Story to Bring you an Important Newsflash!

The voice of the TV newsreader boomed out across the diner.

'And as Moshlings continue to vanish, paws are once again pointing towards arch-criminal Dr. Strangeglove, leading figure in C.L.O.N.C., the Criminal League of Naughty Critters, pictured here with fellow outlaw Sweet Tooth.'

A black and white photograph of the infamous doctor appeared on the screen behind the reporter, and next to that, a mug shot of his sugar-addicted partner-in-crime. The text scrolling across the bottom of the screen read, 'More Moshlings missing.'

'Hey – come to think of it, I haven't seen Gingersnap, Gurgle and Gigi in days,' Roary said, distracted by the content of the news report. Taking out a selection of trading cards, he showed Poppet the ones that had gone missing. 'And those are just the Moshlings beginning with G!'

An anxious expression crossed Roary's face. 'Do you think Strangeglove has them?' – and then, before Poppet could offer an answer – 'Nah – what would he want with my Moshlings . . . '

Roary's roving eyes took in the whole of the diner. 'Now where did our 'gooperstar' get to . . . ?'

Poppet started shooting glances all about her in a sudden state of panic, as Roary set off to find Katsuma.

'Moshlings?! Mr. Snoodle?!' Where had the Moshling gone? 'Snoodle?!'

Hearing a muffled 'Parp!' Poppet caught sight

of him again then. The Silly Snuffler was busy watching TV.

'Ah, Snoodle.'

Katsuma was sitting out back in the diner storeroom.

'Wannabe?' he moaned. 'Ah, what do they know, huh? I've got charisma. I'm the complete package. The real deal.'

Katsuma stood up and started shadow boxing.

'Versatility's my middle name.'

Stanley the Songful Seahorse watched him from where he was bobbing in a sink full of suds, a bored expression on his face.

'You know where I'm coming from . . . doncha?'

Stanley looked at him blankly. He clearly didn't know what to say. But then he was a Songful Seahorse so he couldn't speak. But he could sing, so in reply he started whistling a cheery tune.

Katsuma smiled, his mood lifting. And then he tried to join Stanley in whistling the strangely familiar tune, and that was where it all went wrong. The only sound that came from between Katsuma's lips was a loud and rotten raspberry.

'How d'ya do that?' Katsuma asked Stanley, giving the whistling thing another go.

At that moment, Roary stuck his head around the door. 'Er, everything OK?' he asked, a dozen eyes lighting on Katsuma in the corner, and another two looking at Stanley.

'Uh . . . Hi Yaa Hurricane!' Katsuma shouted, quickly striking a kung fu pose.

'C'mon kid, get it together. We've got a movie to make!' And with that, Roary exited the storeroom again. Katsuma followed immediately; he didn't need telling twice.

Stanley watched them go from his sink of suds. As the storeroom door swung shut behind them, a rubber glove – that until that moment had been lying innocently on the side of the sink – suddenly sprang

to life. Grabbing the Songful Seahorse, it disappeared
as quickly as it had first appeared. And another
Moshling was gone!

CHAPTER SIX

An Egg-cellent Idea

B ack in the diner, Roary and Katsuma joined Poppet and the rest of the gang – Mr. Snoodle, Furi, Luvli, Diavlo and Zommer, with Blinki hovering nearby – who all had their eyes glued to the TV.

Mr. Snoodle started to jump up and down, trumpeting in excitement, as a large egg appeared on the screen. The reporter on the TV was standing next to the egg, which was resting on a cushion inside a large glass case.

'And you join me live here at Bumblechops Manor,'

the reporter was saying, 'where I'm with world-renowned Moshling Collector, Buster Bumblechops, who has just found – yes, I repeat, found – the legendary Great Moshling Egg.'

Mr. Snoodle was going crazy as he stared at the TV.

Buster Bumblechops was sitting in a wheelchair, next to the egg. He looked just a little incapacitated, his legs in plaster and wearing a neck brace.

'Well it was believed the egg was lost forever following the Great Custard Flood of 99999.5,' Buster was saying. 'But as you can see, it's here!'

'What's with him?' Katsuma asked, glancing at the very excitable Mr. Snoodle who was acting nuttier than a Naughty Nutter now.

'Shhhh!' Poppet shushed him, her attention wholly on the television too.

'And could you tell us what might be inside the egg?' the TV reporter asked Buster.

'I'm not entirely sure, but you can bet your fossilized fungus flakes it's one monsterifically mighty Moshling! I'll need all my skills as a master Moshlingologist to hatch it,' the master Moshlingologist explained.

Snoodle was as entranced by the report as Poppet, and was panting after all of his energetic exertions.

'In the wrong paws,' Buster Bumblechops went on, 'the results could be disastrous!'

Snoodle froze on hearing the word 'disastrous', a shocked expression on his yellow face.

'Before I attempt to hatch it at the grand opening of my new, state-of-the-art Moshling sanctuary' – an image of the almost completed sanctuary flashed up on the screen for a moment, before being replaced by a shot of Buster Bumblechops' magnificent home – 'the egg will be on display in my Museum of Moshiness here at Bumblechops Manor.'

'Admission is free,' Buster went on, only now he sounded like he was reading from a cue card, 'thanks to our sponsors at Wobble-ade. Was that all right?' he asked someone off camera as a picture of a bottle of Wobble-ade appeared on the TV.

'It's the fizziest, dizziest soda in town,' went the cheery Wobble-ade jingle.

'Please glug responsibly,' came the voice-over, ending with a loud burp.

'You know what?' Poppet said to Katsuma, as everyone got up to leave, the segment from Bumblechops Manor clearly finished. 'It'd be great to go check out the egg as part of the movie.'

Katsuma had to run to catch up with Roary and the others as they left the diner.

'You know what?' Now it was Katsuma's turn to sound excited. 'It'd be great to go check out the egg as part of the movie.'

Roary looked at Katsuma. 'Now you're thinking like a pro, kid! That's a monsterific idea!'

Roary, Blinki and the rest set off for Bumblechops Manor, leaving Poppet and Snoodle standing on the sidewalk next to Katsuma, who was looking particularly pleased with himself.

'Katsuma!' Poppet snapped, glaring furiously at her friend. 'I can't believe you stole my idea.'

'Hey, take it as a compliment,' Katsuma retorted. 'I only steal from the best. Now, step aside.'

With that, Katsuma ran off after Roary and the others, leaving Poppet and Mr. Snoodle standing at the side of the street, looking crestfallen and confused.

And all the while they were being watched by a periscope poking out of a manhole in the middle of the street.

CHAPTER SEVEN

Secrets in the Sewers

Deep beneath the streets of Monstro City, Flumpy the Pluff was jauntily strolling along a gloomy sewer tunnel. He looked as out of place in the pongy passageway as an Abominable Snowling in the Lost Valley of iSissi. In one hand he was carrying a small paper bag, while Fifi was trapped securely under the other arm.

As he continued on his way through the sewer, he passed various different tunnels signposted with names like 'The Observatory' and 'Submarine to Music Island'. He took a moment to watch a group of Glumps in hard hats digging a tunnel marked 'Bumblechops Manor'.

'Almost there,' Rocko, the head of the team, was saying as Flumpy ambled on his way. 'Just a few more Moshimetres.'

The sewer began to widen out. The Pluff passed a rack stacked with different kinds of gloves. There were rubber gloves, oven gloves, giant foam hands, mittens, boxing gloves, and beard trimmers.

Flumpy hesitated at the entrance to an enormous underground chamber filled with steaming pipes and all manner of wild and weird contraptions.

One wall of the vast room was covered with video monitors, each one displaying an image of a different part of Monstro City. It looked like whoever was in charge here had total CCTV coverage of the whole of the Moshi world.

One of the screens that was relaying images to the sewer-bound base was focused on the sidewalk in front of the diner on Main Street, where Poppet and Katsuma were still bickering.

'You're unbelievable!' Poppet's angry words echoed from the walls of the vaulted subterranean chamber.

'Yeah, I know!' Katsuma said, beaming, clearly not realizing that Poppet's comment had been a criticism rather than a compliment. 'Look, I'm not saying you're wrong . . . You're just not as right as I am.'

Watching the bank of screens – and that one screen in particular – was the sinister silhouette of a frightening figure.

'Mwah-ha. This big-headed fool will be perfect!' the villainous Dr. Strangeglove laughed, as only a moustache-twirling villain can. 'I'm so excited, I could dance!'

Remote control in hand, Strangeglove began channel surfing, flicking past news reports, cookery shows and endless shopping channels.

He paused at a channel showing Zack Binspin's

music video. Moved by the music, the scoundrel couldn't help humming along, and started limbering up with some high kicks.

Hearing someone sniggering from the shadows, Dr. Strangeglove stopped dancing immediately and peered into the gloom at the corners of the room.

Flumpy just stood there, Fifi still under one arm, looking lost and completely out of place at the heart of the villain's underground lair.

'Fishlips? Is that you?' Strangeglove called.

Flumpy gave a shrug and unzipped himself. The now floppy Flumpy costume fell to the floor revealing the Glump who had been hidden inside it all along – Fishlips!

Two other Glumps hurried forward to lead Fifi away, tugging roughly on her lead.

'Must you wear that idiotic disguise every time you run errands?' asked Strangeglove with an exasperated sigh. 'I don't know, what's wrong with a simple nose/spectacles comedy combo?'

Strangeglove pulled out a pair of comedy glasses, complete with a ridiculous false nose attachment, and threw them at Fishlips.

'Sorry boss,' his right-hand Glump apologized. 'It's just so . . . so liberating dressing up as a Moshling! I haven't had that much fun since I went shoplifting in Ooh La Lane and . . .'

'Silence, you babbling ball of buffoonery!' Strangeglove roared. 'I don't pay you to have fun.'

'Er, you don't pay me at all, Doc,' Fishlips pointed out.

'Quite right! Remember, if it weren't for my unparalleled genius as a Glumpodynamicist you'd still be a revolting little Moshling and not a delightfully evil Glump.' Strangeglove gave Fishlips' squelchy cheeks an affectionate pinch. 'Now, did you bring me what I asked for?'

'Oh, sure!' Fishlips said, suddenly remembering the paper bag he was carrying. He tossed it into Strangeglove's hands. 'Throat spray!'

The doctor pulled the spray canister from the bag

and directed a couple of squirts into his mouth, before throwing back his head and gargling with the stuff.

'Mm . . . better,' he began, in a high-pitched squeak before stopping and clearing his throat. 'I mean, better,' he said in his normal villainous voice. 'All that shouting and scheming takes its toll on my throat.'

'Yeah, about that scheme, Doc . . . '

'Scheme? It's more than a mere scheme, my putrid pinkish pal,' Strangeglove said grandly. 'It's a Machiavellian masterpiece of monstrous proportions.'

CHAPTER EIGHT

A Machiavellian
Masterpiece

Fishlips' face creased into an expression of confusion, suggesting that he had no idea what a 'Machiavellian masterpiece' actually was.

Dr. Strangeglove turned to a monitor, which was conveniently running a computer-simulated visualization of his monstrous Machiavellian masterpiece.

'Step one, we poach the Great Moshling Egg from Bumblechops! See what I did there?' he added, twiddling his moustache at what he thought was a clever play on the word 'poach'.

'Step two, when that fame-hungry furball Katsuma

discovers it's gone, he will unwittingly become part of my pernicious plan!

The frown on Fishlips' face deepened. He clearly didn't know what 'pernicious' meant either.

Strangeglove's voice was getting hoarse again, and hoarser by the second. 'Step three, we mobilize our Glump army,' he said, speeding up in an attempt to finish what he had to say before he lost his voice altogether. But it was to no avail, 'and . . . Throat spray!' he croaked.

Fishlips administered another dose of the medicine straight into Strangeglove's mouth.

'What do you think step four might be?' the doctor asked his accomplice in dastardliness, now that his voice had returned. He started to stroke Fishlips as if the Glump was a Tubby Huggishi.

'We buy a lifetime supply of mutant sprouts and retire to a cottage just outside Monstro City?' Fishlips hazarded a guess, filled with hope.

Strangeglove gave the Glump a sharp slap that sent

Fishlips flying. Hitting a nearby monitor with a sink plunger pop, he stuck there for a moment. And then slowly the Glump began to slide down the screen, leaving a trail of gooey drool behind him.

'Step four,' Strangeglove announced, loudly, 'we rule the Swooniverse as—'

'Father and son?' Fishlips suggested.

'No, nano-brain,' Strangeglove snorted. 'As leading members of C.L.O.N.C.!'

Strangeglove gestured towards the wall of monitors. Every single screen was now showing the same image – the C.L.O.N.C. logo, with the Criminal League of Naughty Critters standing in front of it – repeated over and over, right across the whole wall.

'But there's one more thing, Fishlips. In order to make a Glump Army we need Glumps. And what do we need to make Glumps?'

'Twisted morals, rotten values, and a total lack of respect for any . . . '

'No,' Strangeglove corrected his sidekick. 'We need Moshlings.'

At this, he picked up Fifi the Oochie Poochie, holding her in front of Fishlips' face.

Fishlips looked from the terrified puppy to the monstrous machine standing on the other side of the doctor's lair.

The tangle of bubbling vats, rattling conveyor belt and oozing pipes could only be one thing – Dr. Strangeglove's most dastardly invention to date, the Glumpatron 9000 Deluxe. The cavernous holding bulb of the Glumping machine was crammed with cowering Moshlings of every description – everything from Sparkly Sweethearts and Savvy Saplings, to Wheelie YumYums and Potty Pipsqueaks.

'Lots and lots of Moshlings!' Strangeglove cooed before bursting into a bout of maniacal laughter. 'Mwah-ha-ha-haaaa!'

'Glump, Glump, Glump, Glump!' a host of Glumps sang as they bounced their way into the underground lair.

'Doc, we're through!' Rocko called from the head of the line. 'Operation Egg is a go!'

'Then let the Glumping commence!' Strangeglove announced with a showman's flair, as if he were the ringmaster at the Cirque du Moshi.

The villainous mastermind stepped onto a platform, which then began to move through the chamber towards a cage suspended above the Glumpatron 9000.

'The Doctor will see you now,' Strangeglove sniggered as the platform glided upwards, keeping a firm grip on the whimpering Fifi.

'Sneaky, sly and shifty let me introduce myself,

I'm the Doctor they call Strangeglove, a hazard to your health.

I'm here to wreak some mayhem with my terrifying schemes.

And Glump your silly Moshlings with my dastardly machines.'

'*Strangeglove, Strangeglove, they call him Dr. Strangeglove,*' the Glumps chanted as the musical lock securing the cage sprang open. The doctor tossed Fifi inside.

'*Strangeglove, Strangeglove, the one to be afraid of.*
Strangeglove, Strangeglove, they call him Dr. Strangeglove.
Strangeglove, Strangeglove, Strangeglove, Strange.'

'*I assume you think it's sinister to hold an ancient grudge,*' the doctor sang, taking over as the dastardly machine went to work on the Moshlings trapped within, transforming them, one by one, into an army of goo-oozing Glumps.

'*But understand it cost my hand so don't be quick to judge.*
A Musky Husky mangled it and chewed it like a shoe –
He thought it was some sausages so now this glove must do.
Don't impede my evil deeds or try to foil my plans.
Even though I wear this glove I have some helping hands.
So peek outside your window and check behind the door.
Is Dr. Strangeglove lurking or has he called before?'

All of them singing now, Strangeglove and his Glumps set off along the tunnel marked 'Bumblechops Manor', armed with swag bags and the kind of tools a burglar might find useful – hammers, crowbars, glass cutters, the lot.

'Strangeglove, Strangeglove, they call him Dr. Strangeglove. Strangeglove, Strangeglove, the one to be afraid of.'

The Glumps continued to sing as they proceeded along the passageway. Reaching the end of the tunnel, they broke through into the museum wing of Bumblechops Manor. Once inside, they enthusiastically set about vandalizing the display room before finally snatching the Great Moshling Egg that stood in pride of place inside its glass case.

'Strangeglove, Strangeglove, they call him Dr. Strangeglove. Strangeglove, Strangeglove, Strangeglove, Strange.'

Really in the swing of things now, Fishlips pulled out a trombone and accompanied the Glumps' singing with a bit of buzzing brass.

'Let 'em have it, Fishlips!' Strangeglove encouraged the already red-faced Glump. 'Blow harder, you spherical fool!'

'I'll show those Moshis!' Strangeglove laughed, as he watched his minions put his pernicious plan into action. 'Today Monstro City, tomorrow the world!'

CHAPTER NINE

Museum Mayhem

Meanwhile, oblivious to what Dr. Strangeglove and his Glumps were up to in the Museum Wing of Bumblechops Manor, Katsuma, Poppet, Furi, Diavlo, Zommer, Luvli, Roary and Blinki were making their way to Buster's mansion.

'So what happens when we get to Bumblechops Manor?' Katsuma asked the others.

'Our movie begins!' Roary replied, unable to hide the excitement from his voice.

At that moment, the friends arrived outside The Bumblechops Museum of Moshiness, Katsuma trying to barge his way to the front of the queue.

'OK, Blinki? OK, you guys?' Roary said, falling into the role of director with ease. 'Remember, just act natural and smile. And ACTION!'

Blinki zoomed in on Poppet who was holding a microphone. 'Here we are standing in front of Bumblechops . . . '

But before she could finish, Katsuma leapt in front of the hovering eye-camera, elbowing poor Poppet out of shot. 'Welcome to *Katsuma: The Movie*!'

Welcome to Bumblechops Manor!' Poppet shouted, forcing her way back into the shot and rolling her eyes at the camera in despair.

'Keep rolling!' Roary commanded Blinki.

'Here we are,' Katsuma said, butting in again, walking backwards as he talked to reveal the building behind him, 'outside The Bumblechops Museum of Moshiness where . . . Woah!'

Talking and walking at the same time isn't easy,

especially when there's a Silly Snuffler snuffling about behind you. Katsuma didn't see Mr. Snoodle until it was too late. Tripping over the startled Moshling, he actually managed to ring the doorbell before hitting the ground.

As Katsuma landed with a painful thud, the door opened. There sat Buster Bumblechops, still in his wheelchair, with his legs in plaster and wearing the neck brace as he had been on the TV news report.

'Confounded machine!' the Moshlingologist extraordinaire cursed, the wheelchair rolling into the door as he tried – and failed – to control it. 'New-fangled . . .'

He broke off when he saw the monsters standing on his doorstep, a warm look of sheer delight spreading across his face. 'Ah, welcome to my Museum of Moshiness. Come in, come in!'

'Blinki, follow me!' Katsuma said, taking charge and leading the way inside. There was no doubt in his mind which monster was going to be the gooperstar of this movie!

Roary, Poppet and the rest followed the other two inside. As their eyes adjusted after the brilliant sunshine outside, the gang looked more closely at their host.

At first, it looked like he was wriggling in his chair, but then the monsters realized that Buster was surrounded by all manner of Moshlings, and that they were the ones doing the wriggling. There was everything from Warrior Wombats and Fluffy Snugglers to Pilfering Toucans and Fiery Frazzledragons. They were sitting on his lap, climbing on his shoulders and even hiding in the pockets of his clothes.

'Ho, ho, ha ha!' he chuckled. 'That tickles!' Trying hard to ignore the tickling he focused his attention on his newly arrived guests instead. 'You're my first visitors today! Prepare to be amazed!'

Buster pointed a remote control at a door, which bleeped, and then opened, revealing the magnificence of the museum beyond. Only the museum wasn't looking magnificent. The room was wrecked. Totally.

Everyone gasped in horror. Graffiti covered the walls. Exhibits had been smashed and were in ruins, and stinking green goo covered every surface.

A sign that had once read, 'Prehistoric Jessie' had been daubed with paint so that it now read, 'Big Jessie'.

'Oh my! Oh my, my, my!' Buster cried. 'At least the Great Moshling Egg is still here,' he added, his eyes on the glass case at the end of the room.

Mr. Snoodle was already busy snuffling around the room. It was as if he was frantically searching for something.

Poppet couldn't believe her eyes. 'What happened?'

Katsuma, on the other hand, appeared to be unaware of the devastation as he made his way towards the glass case. The rest of the gang uncertainly followed his lead.

Katsuma shooed Mr. Snoodle away from the Great

Moshling Egg. He turned to Blinki. 'Hey, Blinki – are you ready?'

The All-Seeing Moment Muncher winked and started recording.

'Here I am with the legendary Great Moshling Egg,' Katsuma began his piece to camera, but then broke off almost immediately.

Mr. Snoodle was going crazy now. It was very off-putting for the gooperstar-in-the-making. 'Snoodle!'

Having shooed Snoodle away again, he turned back to Blinki. 'Here I am with the legendary Great Moshling Egg . . . '

Katsuma paused again. None of the others were paying him any attention. Luvli, Poppet, Furi, Diavlo, Zommer, Buster and Roary were all wandering around the museum in a daze.

For the first time, Katsuma bothered to look where the others were looking, and slowly it dawned on him that the room had been wrecked.

Shocked, he put out a hand to support himself and touched the egg. 'Which is, er . . .'

With a gloopy popping sound, the egg abruptly turned round, changing shape as it did so.

'A Glump!?' Poppet exclaimed in horror, staring at the squidgy thing that a moment ago everyone had taken to be the Great Moshling Egg.

Making curious grunting noises, the Glump jumped off the plinth and squidged away as the harsh klaxon roar of an alarm blared throughout the museum wing of Bumblechops Manor.

'Keep rolling,' Roary ordered Blinki. 'This is dynamite! Dynamite!'

A tooting parp from Mr. Snoodle made everyone look round in surprise. The Silly Snuffler had found something. It was a business card, and not just any business card – it was Dr. Strangeglove's business card.

'Parp!' Snoodle tooted and then jumped back in surprise as a holographic image of Dr. Strangeglove sprang out of the card. Standing next to the flickering holographic Strangeglove was his right-hand Glump, Fishlips.

And then the holographic Strangeglove began to speak. 'Greetings, fur-brained egg-lovers! It is I, Dr. Strangeglove, and it is I who have taken . . . temporary ownership of the Great Moshling Egg. **Mwa-ha-haaaaa-haaaaaa!**'

CHAPTER TEN

Mission Improbable

'**M**wa-ha-haaaaa-haaaaaa!' Dr. Strangeglove's evil laughter echoed across Monstro City, booming from every TV set and every Blaring Boombox, relayed via Blinki's live video feed.

Monsters everywhere spat out their tea in shock, fell off their chairs in amazement and even nibbled their hands instead of their toast.

Inside the devastated museum wing of Bumblechops Manor, Katsuma, Luvli, Diavlo, Furi, Zommer, Poppet, Roary Scrawl and Buster Bumblechops himself gawped at the holographic double act as Strangeglove continued to outline his latest dastardly scheme.

'And I will obliterate it into a billion bitty bits . . . '

'Great villain-y wordplay, boss,' Fishlips leered.

'Shush, you simpering, overgrown meatball,' Strangeglove snapped. 'Now where was I? Oh yes . . . Into a billion bitty bits unless I receive three items!'

'How about a sensible hat, a moustache trimmer and a decent tailor?' Luvli whispered in Poppet's ear.

'I'm a collector of rare Moshi artefacts not fusty old eggs,' the hologram went on. 'Bring me . . . A packet of microwavable Oobla Doobla, the freshly cried tears of a Blue Jeepers Moshling, and finally, the mythical Frosted Rainbow Rox.

'And here's the really devious bit,' the villain chuckled. 'For dramatic effect and maximum inconvenience, I want all three items at the peak of Mount Sillimanjaro by midnight!'

To add extra emphasis to his words, the hologram of Dr. Strangeglove brought his fist down hard on his holographic sidekick. Fishlips was splatted flat but only for a moment before returning to his normal meatball shape.

'Midnight?!' Katsuma and Poppet exclaimed in unison.

'Yes, midnight. Exactly twelve hours from now. Tick tock, tick tock,' Strangeglove taunted them, holding up a panicky looking Mini Ben. Unable to help himself, the Teeny Tick Tock chimed the hour of noon. 'Happy hunting. And remember, all three items by midnight or the egg gets it!'

The hologram crackled and in the next moment fizzled out completely, zipping back into the business card, which promptly transformed into a briefcase. The lid of the briefcase popped open, revealing three sections, each one clearly intended for one of the three artefacts Strangeglove had demanded that the monsters find for him.

Keeping all his eyes on the case, just in case it suddenly decided to turn into something else, Roary closed the lid. 'Well whaddya know? It's an open and shut kidnap case!'

Buster Bumblechops was too distracted and distraught to appreciate Roary's terrible joke. 'Oobla Doobla? Tears? No, he couldn't . . . he . . . oh my . . . '

Buster rolled himself out of the room, hitting the door frame on the way out. 'Oof! Uh! Ah!' And then he was gone.

'Well, that was interesting,' Katsuma said, looking into the flabbergasted faces of his friends. 'Now, let's get back to our movie.'

Everyone else stared at him, their flabbergasted expressions not going anywhere.

'How can you think about the movie when Strangeglove's got the Great Moshling Egg?' Poppet scolded him.

'Besides, the movie's been cancelled,' Roary declared.

Katsuma froze, in a state of shock. He couldn't believe what his long ears were hearing. 'Cancelled?!' This was the worst news . . . ever!

'Yeah, egg-stenuating circumstances! This whole kidnap thing is red hot news; Blinki and I have gotta follow whoever's bone-headed . . . I mean brave enough to get those artefacts. Come on, Blinki, let's go.'

'Wait a minute!' Poppet cried out, stopping Roary in his tracks. 'We have to rescue the Egg!'

Mr. Snoodle nodded furiously in agreement.

'Darling, have you lost your mind?' Luvli swooned.

'Finding those artefacts will be harder than nailing goo to the wall,' Diavlo pointed out.

Unseen by the others, Zommer gathered up some of the goo the Glumps had left behind and then pulled a nail out of his head. Taking a hammer from his pocket, he successfully managed to nail some of the goo to the wall at his first attempt, although it promptly fell off again

'Wait! Wait! I've got an idea!' Katsuma announced, jumping up and down in an attempt to get Blinki's attention. 'We'll collect the stuff Strangeglove wants and rescue the egg. And when I say 'we', I kinda mean me!'

Safe in their subterranean lair, Dr. Strangeglove and Fishlips observed the events unfolding at Bumblechops Manor on one of the many screens that made up the monitor wall.

Katsuma was still speaking. 'But I guess you can all tag along to help carry . . .'

'Your ego, darling?' Luvli interrupted.

Katsuma scowled. ' . . . Supplies and to give me a hand along the way.'

'Let's tell Mr Bumblechops,' Poppet said.

Strangeglove watched as the pink-furred monster headed off after the wheelchair-bound Buster.

'Haha! What did I tell you, Fishlips?'

The Glump stared at the doctor with a look of intense concentration on his face. 'To exfoliate twice a week . . . '

'No, you rotund roulade! That self-centred catty critter took the bait. It's all going according to plan.' He burst into another bout of crazed laughter just as, on the screen, Katsuma slipped in a puddle of goo and fell over, before picking himself up and following his friends.

'Captain Pong!' Strangeglove shouted and the Glump in question appeared on another of the monitor screens. 'Fire up *ScareForce One*!'

And so, at the centre of a vast footprint-shaped valley, a battalion of Glumps boarded C.L.O.N.C.'s *ScareForce One*. Its engines running up to speed, the gigantic airship slowly lifted off.

The Moshis were in trouble now!

CHAPTER ELEVEN

The Terrible Truth

'He's going to hatch the egg?!' the entire gang shouted as one.

They were standing in the imposing Grand Library of Bumblechops Manor. Books covered every wall, while floor to ceiling ladders set on casters flanked either side of the room. In the middle of the room stood a table and on top of this was a model of the new Moshling Sanctuary. Beside the window sat a globe of the Moshi world.

Buster was busy searching his shelves of old books as

best he could – considering his legs were in plaster, his neck was in a brace, and he was stuck in his wheelchair.

'Now where did I put that journal?' he was muttering to himself. 'That's not it . . . No! Not this one . . . Ah! Here it is . . . No . . . I know it's here somewhere . . . '

'But how?' Katsuma asked. He was still in a state of shock at Buster's revelation that the mad doctor was planning to hatch the Great Moshling Egg. 'Aren't you the only one who can hatch an egg this ancient?'

'Yes,' Buster replied, 'but theoretically someone could hatch it by applying three special ingredients.'

Katsuma looked mystified. 'Really?'

'Let me guess,' Poppet said, her forehead furrowed in concentration, 'Microwavable Oobla Doobla, tears from a Blue Jeepers and the Frosted Rainbow Rox.'

'Uh . . . yeah,' agreed Katsuma, eager to appear as if he knew what was going on. 'That's exactly what I was going to say.'

'But then what?' chipped in Furi.

'Don't you see?' Buster sounded exasperated, as if he had reached the end of his tether. 'Once hatched, a Moshling this ancient could be transformed into a monstrously powerful Glump!'

'And . . . ?' Katsuma asked, clearly confused.

'And then Strangeglove will use this Mega Glump to lead a Glump Army to destroy Monstro City.'

A strained silence fell over all present in the Grand Library.

'So . . . We can't give him those artefacts.'

'But if we don't, he'll smash the egg,' Poppet pointed out in distress.

'This is sensational!' Roary muttered, furiously scribbling in his notepad.

'Some-Moshi will have to get those artefacts and rescue the egg,' Buster announced, stating the facts as clearly as he could so that no one was in any doubt as to what would have to happen next.

Katsuma threw a nod Blinki's way, smiling smugly. This was the chance he'd been waiting for.

'Not just some-Moshi,' he said. 'This Moshi! Me! The whole world is relying on . . . ' He sprang into action, making sure Blinki got his best side, while trying out his trademark kung fu move. 'Hi Yaa Hurricane!' With one powerful kick, he sent the globe flying from its frame. Katsuma!'

The globe bounced off a bookcase and collided with the orange monster, sending him flying into a pile of books.

'Don't worry, Mr Bumblechops,' Poppet said, 'we'll collect the artefacts and use 'em to lure Strangeglove into our trap.'

'Trap? What trap?' asked Katsuma, emerging from beneath the pile of books.

Poppet returned his look. 'We'll think of something.'

Pulling out an old map from a tube, Buster unrolled it on the table, next to the model of the Moshling Sanctuary.

'Your first stop,' he said, pointing at a spot on the map, 'is the Gombala Gombala Jungle!'

'Whoa! How are we gonna get there by midnight?' asked Zommer, who was distractedly trying to squeeze Blinki into his empty eye-socket. 'By the time we get there we'll have forgotten what we . . . er, I forgot . . .'

'Don't worry,' Buster said. He rolled himself over to the huge French windows that looked out over the manor's formal gardens, and flung them open. 'It's easy if you whistle! Katsuma?'

Everyone looked in Katsuma's direction. Overwhelmed by the pressure of the moment, knowing that he couldn't whistle for toffee – or Sludge Fudge for that matter – he pretended he was busy shadow boxing. He looked up, acting like he was surprised to see his friends staring at him.

'Say what?'

'You need to whistle,' said Poppet. 'Like this.'

Putting her fingers to her lips Poppet gave an almighty, deafening whistle. As the monsters recovered and the echoes of the shrill whistle faded, the monsters became aware of the distant waka-waka of rotor blades.

As the sound drew nearer, shielding their eyes from the bright Moshi sun with their hands, the monsters peered into the sky and saw a flock of Twirly Tiddlycopters zooming towards Bumblechops Manor.

Roary watched the Tiddlycopters approaching with sweat beading on his brow and swaying slightly, a nervous look in all of his eyes.

'Er, did I mention I'm afraid of flying?' he said weakly, pulling at his collar as his eyes began to spin.

The Twirly Tiddlycopters were now hovering directly overhead, the down draft of their whirling rotors making trees bend and sending fur flying.

'Blinki!' Roary shouted to be heard over the roar of the Twirly Tiddlycopters. 'I hereby promote you to Chief Roving Reporter at Large. Enjoy!'

Zommer leant forward and gave Blinki a congratulatory slap on the back of his gleaming

Moshling-cam case.

The Twirly Tiddlycopters lowered a huge basket between them. The gang all climbed in – Mr. Snoodle cradled in Poppet's arms. All, that is, except for Buster and Roary. Katsuma stood at the front of the basket, posing for Blinki.

'Here,' Buster shouted, 'take this! It's my great uncle Furbert Snufflepeeps' Moshi journal!'

'Thank you, Mr Bumblechops,' Poppet shouted back, gladly accepting the leather-bound book from him.

'Call me Buster. And remember, as Uncle Furbert used to say . . . Katsuma? Are you listening?'

Katsuma looked round.

'"If you stand for nothing, you'll fall for anything!" Good luck! The entire Moshi World is relying on you!'

'No pressure then,' Roary muttered to no Moshi in particular.

The basket lifted off, towed by the flock of Twirly Tiddlycopters, Buster and Roary waving the friends farewell as the monsters' peculiar transport disappeared over the horizon.

Log in to **MOSHIMONSTERS.COM**, click the **ENTER SECRET CODE** button and type the **forth word** on the **tenth line** on **page 49**. Your surprise free gift will appear in your treasure chest!

CHAPTER TWELVE

Jungle High Jinks

I t was hot and humid in the Gombala Gombala Jungle, but then it was always hot and humid in the Gombala Gombala Jungle. Cheeky Chimps swung through the trees, while the cries of Pilfering Toucans carried across the leafy canopy.

The gang were in the middle of the jungle, at the very heart of darkness, surrounded by thick foliage.

While the other monsters were staring at the Cheeky Chimps swinging from one branch to the next high above, like a troupe of particularly hairy Moshilympic gymnasts, Poppet had her head buried in the book Buster Bumblechops had given her.

'According to Snufflepeeps' journal, Microwavable Oobla Doobla can only be found here.'

Katsuma peered over her shoulder. 'Where?'

Poppet pointed at a drawing of a village on the page in front of her.

'Here. Right in the middle of the . . . '

'Woolly Blue Hoodoo Village!' Poppet and Katsuma said at the same time, Poppet shaking in her boots, Katsuma sounding less like a hero and more like a zero.

Right on cue, the pounding of drums drifted through the jungle. Katsuma turned to address Blinki's blinking camera eye.

'I . . . sorry, we,' he quickly corrected himself, 'are about to head into the depths of the jungle, risking my life to bag the first artefact. Onward!'

Picking up the briefcase, Katsuma turned and walked slap bang into a tree. Once the mini-solar system of stars had stopped orbiting his head, Katsuma picked himself up and tried again, leading the way ever deeper into the jungle.

The others had little choice but to tag along after him, Furi, Diavlo and Luvli at the front. Poppet, Zommer and Snoodle brought up the rear, Zommer strumming away on his air guitar, while Poppet read to Snoodle from Furbert Snufflepeeps' journal.

'It says here these Woolly Blue Hoodoos communicate mostly by whistling. Whaddya think of that, Snoodle?'

Poppet looked up from the book. Katsuma, Furi, Luvli, Blinki and Diavlo had vanished.

'Hey! Where'd they all go?'

Poppet watched as Mr. Snoodle started sniffing around the jungle plants. He froze, his snout wrinkling. He'd picked up a scent.

'C'mon, Zommer!' Poppet exclaimed excitedly. 'This way!'

'Say what? Eleventy past seven?' Zommer said, a

dazed expression on his stitched-up, one-eyed face. 'Man, I gotta tune up!'

Meanwhile, in another part of the jungle, Katsuma, Luvli, Furi, Diavlo and Blinki found themselves in a village of mud and straw huts that looked a lot like the picture in Furbert Snufflepeeps' journal.

This was the source of the drumming too, the tribal rhythms setting Katsuma's toes tapping. The friends advanced a little more cautiously than before, eyes peeled for the treasure they had come all this way to find.

'There it is!' Katsuma hissed, eyes wide with delight. He'd found it! 'Microwavable Oobla Doobla! Let's go!'

'But what about Poppet and Zommer?' Diavlo said, realizing the party had become separated.

'Look, if they can't keep up it's not my fault,' Katsuma grunted defensively, noticing Luvli's disapproving look.

Apparently happy that he had done enough to excuse

himself, Katsuma turned to Blinki. 'In a dramatic twist, two of my brave assistants are missing!'

'Two and a half, if you count Mr. Snoodle,' Luvli pointed out.

'Oh yeah . . . '

Katsuma sighed, casting his eyes to the jungle depths once more as it finally struck him how worried he was about his friends. And then something else struck him. It was an idea.

'Oh yeah! Don't sweat it,' he told Luvli. 'Snoodle will sniff us out, no problem.'

'Sweat it?' Luvli huffed. 'Darling, please! Zommer sweats; I glow!'

The sound of the drums became louder and merged with the rumble of chanting voices. The friends stood there, dumbfounded, as a tribe of Moshlings – that were little more than bright blue balls of fur, horns and face paint – emerged from the huts and surrounded them.

'Gombala Gombala walla walla hoohaa. Gombala

Gombala walla walla hoohaa,' the curious creatures chanted as they surrounded the monsters.

'Don't worry,' said Katsuma, taking charge, 'I've got this covered.'

A creature that was clearly the chief of the tribe – going by his interesting choice of headgear – appeared from out of the crowd. He was holding his skull-topped staff before him with a furious scowl on his furry face, as if to say, 'I'm the chief. Don't mess with the best.'

Katsuma approached the chief, Blinki buzzing after him.

The Woolly Blue Hoodoo gave an inquisitive whistle, as if to say, 'Wassup?'

Katsuma stopped dead in his tracks. He didn't know what to do.

'He wants you to whistle,' Luvli called out. 'Go on, darling – pucker up!'

Steeling himself, Katsuma took a deep breath and brought his lips together in a puckered pout. But rather than a shrill whistle, when he blew, what came out was a rather pathetic, and rather wet, raspberry.

Even through all the blue fur, the look of bewilderment on the chief's face was plain to see.

The leader of the tribe whistled again, more insistently this time.

Katsuma smiled at his friends, giving them a wave and an 'I told you so' wink, as the Woolly Blue Hoodoos closed in around them.

CHAPTER THIRTEEN

In a Stew

'Listen!' Poppet said excitedly, turning to Zommer and Snoodle. The drums were getting louder now. 'We're almost there!'

Not far away, underneath the tree where the Microwavable Oobla Doobla grew, Luvli and Katsuma were deep in conversation.

'"Don't worry, I've got this covered?"' Luvli was saying, repeating Katsuma's words back to him. 'Honestly, darling, you've dropped us right in the soup!'

'Actually, I think it's more of a stew,' Furi said,

dipping a claw into the bubbling broth, 'although it might be a cassoulet!'

Whatever it was, the friends were sitting in a large cauldron full of the stuff. Or, to put it another way, they were up to their necks in it!

The Woolly Blue Hoodoos – who were clearly feeling a little on the peckish side – were dancing around the cauldron.

Furi was also feeling a little peckish. The smell of the stew was making his mouth water. Putting a napkin around his neck, he picked up an onion, as it floated past, and started to peel it. Ladle in hand, he scooped up some of the gravy and basted himself with it, smiling as if he was enjoying a hot bath.

Picking up another onion, he was surprised when it gave a cough, blinked, and then struggled to rise into the air where it then stayed, hovering above the cauldron. It wasn't an onion, it was Blinki.

'Look, how was I to know these little critters were so attached to their Oobla Doobla?' complained

Katsuma, coming over all defensive again.

'What's that?' Luvli started, hearing a loud whistle come from somewhere nearby.

At that moment, Poppet wandered into the village, her head still stuck in the book she was carrying. The chanting and the drums stopped. The silence that followed was worse than the chanting and drumming that had gone before.

The chief strode forward into Poppet's path.

'Excuse me, Poppet?' Katsuma called from the cauldron. 'I've got everything under control!'

'Really?'

'Sure! They're just, er, having us for dinner.'

Poppet puckered her lips and whistled at the chief. The chief whistled back.

'I think he said we can have the Oobla Doobla if we go lowest in the limbo!' Poppet called to her friends. The others just stared at her in awestruck amazement.

Katsuma looked the most awestruck and bewildered of them all. 'The what-bo?'

'Whatever they do, I hope they hurry,' panted Diavlo. 'Even I'm getting hot in here!'

The chief nodded and two of the Hoodoos held up a limbo pole between them while another Hoodoo, who looked every part the Hoodoo Limbo Dancing Champion, stepped up to do his thing. The Hoodoo drums began to beat again.

The Champion approached the limbo pole and, bending over backwards, passed beneath without any problems at all. A cheer went up from the tribe.

Now it was Poppet's turn. Stepping up to the limbo pole, the monsters' intense stares upon her, she shuffled forward, hoping to pass under the pole without touching it herself.

Keeping her eyes on the pole she too shuffled underneath. The smile that lit up her face as she successfully made it to the other side without disturbing the bar said it all.

But the Hoodoos weren't done yet. The bar lowered

a notch, the Champion stepped forward again . . . and passed clear underneath, again!

Steeling herself, Poppet prepared to meet the Champion's challenge. You could have cut the atmosphere with a small vegetable knife.

It was a valiant effort, and for a moment it looked like she might actually make it, but then, at the very last moment, a quiff of fur caught the pole and sent it rattling to the ground.

'Sorry, I just couldn't stoop that low,' Poppet apologised, surfacing again after being thrown into the hot stew by the unimpressed Hoodoos.

'Now what?' grumped Katsuma.

'That's what!' Luvli declared. The others followed her gaze.

Zommer was preparing to take his turn at challenging the Champion Hoodoo Limbo Dancer.

It didn't seem fair; the Hoodoos had set the bar very low. Zommer looked at it, one eyebrow raised, and then waved his hands indicating he wanted it set lower still! What was he thinking?

The chief and his Hoodoos laughed at Zommer's foolish bravado as the monster approached the limbo bar. The laughter soon stopped, however, as Zommer calmly detached his head and – removing one of his legs to use as a golf club – knocked it under the bar. The rest of his body followed, shuffling under using only one foot!

Safely on the other side – as the chief applauded his grand effort and the former Champion Limbo Dancer was escorted away in tears – Zommer put himself together again.

At a whistle from the chief, one of the Hoodoos tugged on a chain dangling over the side of the cauldron and pulling out the plug. The bubbling stew had soon drained out of the huge cooking pot. With the aid of a ladder, Luvli, Diavlo, Furi, Poppet and

Katsuma climbed out.

'Come on,' Poppet said, shaking bits of carrot out of her fur, 'let's go!'

'Nice one, Zommer!' Diavlo cheered.

'Do we leave a tip?' Luvli asked.

Furi looked at the others disappointedly. 'No dessert?'

The chief proudly presented Zommer with the prize they had trekked all that way to find – the Microwavable Oobla Doobla – which he promptly passed to Poppet. Opening the briefcase, she placed the Oobla Doobla carefully inside. 'One down, two to go!'

'Let's get out of here!' said Katsuma, ready to embark upon the next leg of their quest.

'Toodle-hoodoo!' Zommer waved to his new friends.

Katsuma grabbed the case and immediately started to shake. The briefcase was vibrating. Lights like tired Twistmas tree decorations lit up around its edge, framing a TV screen that everyone could now see was built into its side.

'Mwah-hahahaha!' Strangeglove's all too familiar

moustachioed face laughed at them from the screen. 'Congratulations, my monstery minions! As you can see, I'm also on the case! Mwa-ha!'

'Mwa-ha!' came Fishlips' voice, echoing his master's maniacal mirth.

'Silence, felonious falafel!' Strangeglove snapped. 'Tick tock, tick tock,' he said, taunting the Moshis again, 'better hurry. I like my Jeepers' tears freshly wept and my frosted Rainbow Rox served slightly sub-zero. Try saying that after a few Wobble-ades.'

Behind him, Fishlips obediently glugged some Wobble-ade. 'Frosted Rainbow Rox served slightly sub-zero frosted rainbow sox rightly . . . ' he said before Strangeglove silenced him by clamping a hand over his mouth.

'Now run along and remember . . . ' – the evil mastermind tried to pull his hand free of Fishlips' mouth again, but found his sidekick stuck there as surely as if he had been glued on with Glump goo – 'Sillimanjaro by midnight, or else!'

Strangeglove's bullying broadcast complete, the lights winked out and the briefcase returned to normal. Mr. Snoodle gave it a wary sniff, just to be sure.

Katsuma carefully picked it up again. 'Hi Yaa Hurricane!' he exclaimed, striking a suitably heroic pose for Blinki.

He just hoped that all his posturing was hiding the fact that, deep down inside, he couldn't have felt more afraid.

CHAPTER FOURTEEN

The Next Arm and a Leg

The monsters' walk back through the jungle was a much more relaxed affair than it had been when they were heading towards the Hoodoo village. Now that the immediate danger had passed, Katsuma was feeling a lot more relaxed about what had happened.

Risking walking backwards again, Katsuma was talking directly to Blinki. ' . . . And then I was almost boiled alive by a group of vicious savages, but I've led us to safety with my uncanny sixth sense that . . . '

Katsuma paused and looked down. He was standing

in mid-air. Not looking where he was going, he had managed to walk right off the edge of a cliff.

'Waahhhhhhhh!' he said, as he plunged from view and into a river far below. Surfacing again, shaking a Batty Bubblefish off the top of his head, he called up to his friends who were still standing safely at the edge of the precipice. 'Blinki, did you get that?'

The Batty Bubblefish surfaced again then as well, and squirted a jet of water into Katsuma's face, just to make sure he understood how unhappy it was about the situation too.

'Now what?' Poppet sounded weary as she watched Katsuma being carried away by the current.

Luvli turned to Diavlo and Blinki. The only ones who could fly, the three of them were hovering a few Moshimetres above the ground. 'I'll take Poppet and Snoodle – you two take Furi and Zommer.'

'Giddyup!' shouted Furi enthusiastically, as he jumped on top of Blinki.

Grabbing Zommer's hand, Diavlo followed Luvli

and Blinki as they glided over the edge of the cliff with their passengers, Blinki wobbling under Furi's weight. 'Hold on tight, Zom . . . ' the hothead said as he glided down the side of the cliff, gripping Zommer's hand tightly.

It was only when he actually glanced back a few moments later that he saw that the rest of Zommer's body wasn't attached to his hand.

'Oh well, he did say he'd give his right arm to be this high!'

By the time the others joined him, by the side of the river, apart from looking bedraggled and being more than a little wet, Katsuma was delighted.

'I hope you got that, Blinki,' he said, strutting up and down at the water's edge. 'I obviously do all my own stunts.'

'Forget about that!' Diavlo said, clearly concerned. 'Zommer's vanished.'

'At least he's armless!' Katsuma winked at Blinki.

'Katsuma!' Poppet cried.

'Look, we can't go back for him now,' Katsuma said trying to defend himself in the face of Poppet's furious reaction. 'Rockers like Zommer know how to look after themselves.'

Back at the top of the cliff, Zommer gazed distractedly around him as the others set off again on the next leg of their quest. One of the Woolly Blue Hoodoos from the village came up to him and offered him a drink from CocoLoco.

Accepting the gift, slurping Bongo Colada from the top of the Naughty Nutter through a straw, Zommer followed the Hoodoo back to the village where a celebration party was in full swing. A host of Hoodoos and Naughty Nutters were dancing the conga and everyone present was clearly having a walla-walla-hoohaa time. There was only one thing missing, as far as Zommer was concerned. He looked longingly at the stump of his missing arm.

His new friend fished an arm out of the cauldron and handed it to Zommer who slotted it into place giving the Hoodoo a grin and a double thumbs up. It was a perfect fit.

'Besides, time is running out!' Katsuma finished.

'Well I don't like leaving him,' Poppet pressed, trying to stay angry at Katsuma, 'but for once you might be right.' She was still poring over the book. 'I think it's time to go to Jollywood to get us some Blue Jeepers' tears!'

'It's time to go to Jollywood to get us some Blue Jeepers' tears,' Katsuma repeated for Blinki's benefit and set off, heading in the wrong direction.

'Katsuma!' Poppet sighed in exasperation. 'This way!'

A periscope popped up from out of the river and watched them go.

BUSTER BUMBLECHOPS discovers the **GREAT MOSHLING EGG** hidden in the ruins of an ancient temple, deep in the Gombala Gombala Jungle. It's the treasure he has been seeking!

DR. STRANGEGLOVE
and his fiendish Glumps trash
the Museum of Moshiness
at Bumblechops Manor and
steal the **GREAT MOSHLING EGG!**

Unfortunately for the
Moshi Monsters, Microwavable
Oobla Doobla can only be found in
one very dangerous place - the
WOOLLY BLUE HOODOO VILLAGE!

Deep in his secret sewer lair, Dr. Strangeglove watched as the monsters went on their way. 'Run along, my artefact gathering goons! Haha!'

'Uh, boss,' Fishlips said, clearly nervous about pointing out a potential spanner in the works of the doctor's pernicious plan, 'did you know Katsuma would be bringing his pals along?'

'Not exactly.' Strangeglove began to pace up and down before the bank of monitors. 'And I've no doubt Katsuma will try to outsmart me. That's why I have ordered Sweet Tooth to take steps . . . deliciously sugary steps, to ensure Katsuma's friends are . . . conveniently side-tracked.'

CHAPTER FIFTEEN

Candy Cane Chaos

'No, I've always seen myself as an action hero; a maverick operating outside the system,' Katsuma said as he and Luvli, Poppet, Furi, Diavlo, Snoodle and Blinki continued their trek through the sweaty depths of the Gombala Gombala Jungle, 'an enigmatic loner who . . .'

Furi suddenly stopped. 'Wha-ha!'

'What it is?' Katsuma asked.

Furi was looking at a tiny top hat-shaped sweet that was lying on the ground. It was only the first of a trail of sweets, wending between the trees.

'Should I or shouldn't I?' Furi was debating with himself.

'Careful, Furi!' Poppet said, pointing to a page in the book. 'The journal says this area is extremely dangerous!'

Furi picked up a candy flower and scoffed it. 'Not dangerous – delicious!'

'Ah, journal shmournal. It looks pretty sweet to me.' Katsuma shot Blinki a wink.

The friends set off, following the trail of candies, until they came to a spot where there was a small pile of sweets waiting for them.

'Stop, everyone!' Poppet shouted. 'Wait!'

Furi stopped to pick up the sweets, causing the rest of the monsters to run into him. It was then that the ground gave way beneath them.

'Aaaargh!' the friends screamed.

As they plunged into the trap, they were watched by two blank-eyed miners.

'Didn't they say to leave the orange one?' one of them said to the other.

'Yeah, but I'm colour blind. And stupid. And I wasn't really listening,' the other replied. 'Who cares? We're hypnotized.'

'True!' agreed the first hypnotised miner.

Now underground, the friends found themselves hurtling down a spiralling slide. The slide entered a tunnel and then spewed the Moshis out on the side, into the collecting funnel of a huge sweet-making machine.

There was a ping and the monsters emerged, travelling by conveyor belt now. Each of them was trapped inside a sweet sugar shell.

'Hehehehe!' an evil, high-pitched cackle echoed around the cavernous caves where the friends now found themselves. 'Looks like you're in one heck of a sticky situation!'

Poppet shot anxious glances about the cave. 'Oh no, isn't that . . .'

'Sweet Tooth!' Furi gulped fearfully.

'Ain't life sweet!' screeched the maniac monster.

Suddenly the caves were filled with a foot stomping music as more hypnotized miners appeared from tunnel mouths or on rocky ledges, and began to sing.

'Sweet Tooth HEY! Sweet Tooth HEY! Sweet Tooth HEY! Sweet Tooth HEY!

Stomp to the beat here's a sweet candy treat,

There's a new kinda baddie in town.

Pink fluffy hair with a mind-blowing stare,

And a face like a maniac clown.

Sweet Tooth HEY! Sweet Tooth HEY! Sweet Tooth HEY! Sweet Tooth HEY!

Goody goody gumdrops,

Heat seekin' lollipops,

Fizz bombs 'n' treacly goo.

Lemonade grenades,

Lotsa sherbet cavalcades,

And a gobstoppin' bubblegum chew.'

'I'm gonna hit you with a volley from my kaleidoscopic lolly!' Sweet Tooth shouted as the miners sang on.

'Stomp to the beat, here's a sweet candy treat,
There's a new kinda baddie in town.
Pink fluffy hair with a mind-blowing stare,
And a face like a maniac clown.
STOP!
Wonder why,
You've got the urge to eat ten tons of pie.
Well maybe you've been hypnotized, kaleidobopped and mesmerized
So run away faster, escape that swirling blaster.'
'Ain't life sweet!' Sweet Tooth's voice echoed around the cavern, making the Moshis start in fear.

'Stomp to the beat here's a sweet candy treat,
There's a new kinda baddie in town.
Pink fluffy hair with a mind-blowing stare,

And a face like a maniac clown.

Goody goody gumdrops,

Heat seekin' lollipops,

Fizz bombs 'n' treacly goo,

Lemonade grenades,

Lotsa sherbet cavalcades,

And a gobstoppin' bubblegum chew.

Stomp to the beat here's a sweet candy treat,

There's a new kinda baddie in town.

Pink fluffy hair with a mind-blowing stare,

And a face like a maniac clown.'

'I'm mad, bad and dangerous to slurp!' Sweet Tooth

cried triumphantly.

CHAPTER SIXTEEN

Rollercoaster Ride

While Sweet Tooth and his mesmerized miner minions were busy singing and stomping, Diavlo was getting distinctly hot under the collar. In fact he got so hot his sugar shell melted!

Sweet Tooth was too busy enjoying himself to notice as Diavlo bundled his friends into the procession of waiting sweet carts, their sugar shells shattering as they landed in the wagons. With a blast of volcano power, Diavlo set the mine carts rolling along their tracks and away through the Candy Cane Caves.

It was only then that the self-obsessed sugar-mad

villain realized that Strangeglove's prey were getting away.

'Barfmallows! Where are they going?' Sweet Tooth shrieked.

Activating a button on his lollipop blaster, Sweet Tooth summoned his *Candy Cruiser*. Leaping on board the pod, grabbing the controls, he sped off after the escaping Moshis.

'Please keep your paws inside the carriages at all times!' Sweet Tooth's manic laughter chased the monsters through the mine as the villain opened up with the cruiser's lemonade grenade launcher.

Mr. Snoodle unintentionally caught one of the candy bombs in his mouth before Poppet pulled it out and hurled it at the approaching *Candy Cruiser*. The grenade splurged against the front of the pod, sending Sweet Tooth into a wild loop the loop.

The trucks rolled over a rise and took off down the other side, quickly picking up speed.

The three carts carrying the monsters separated as they crested the rise. Katsuma, alone in the lead cart, red into a gaping, sticky tunnel mouth first. He was soon followed by Poppet, Snoodle and Furi in the second carriage, with Diavlo and Luvli bringing up the rear in the last of the thundering trucks.

Back in control of his cruiser, Sweet Tooth pursued them into the tunnel. Just as he was beginning to close on the Moshis again, the cruiser's built-in videophone began to ring and Dr. Strangeglove's face appeared on the screen.

'Remember, let the orange catty thing escape!'

'Roger and out!' Sweet Tooth said.

At the flick of another switch on the rogue's lollipop, a cluster of liquorice wheels went rolling across the track. The last one hit Diavlo and Luvli's carriage, knocking it onto an adjoining, parallel track. The two monsters watched as Sweet Tooth went after their friends.

It was only as the others disappeared into yet

another tunnel that they saw the planks barring the way ahead. Their hands raised before their faces, the cart smashed through the boards and bounced off a giant jelly, launching Luvli and Diavlo through the hole in an enormous doughnut to land on top of a humongous ice cream.

'Great lava lumps, that was a close call,' Diavlo gasped breathlessly, dashing off immediately and running straight into a wall.

A dull droning sound filled the air and a dark shadow fell across the friends. Luvli looked up, swallowed hard, and gave Diavlo a nudge. 'You ever get one of those days when things just don't pan out?'

'Uh-oh . . . ' Diavlo said, as a thick suction pipe descended from the airship-shaped shadow that was now blotting out the sun above them.

Meanwhile, Sweet Tooth was closing on the other carts. Pointing his lollipop at the entrance to another tunnel he activated yet another trap. Gigantic lollipops began to swing back and forth across the tracks as the carriage carrying Poppet, Snoodle and Furi hurtled after Katsuma's cart.

But when the friends managed to evade the trap, at Sweet Tooth's command, sherbert cannons fired. Their liquorice-stick missiles rocketed over the heads of the Furi, Poppet and Snoodle, striking a lollipop signal and changing the points on the track.

As Katsuma headed left, the others were sent round to the right. But thanks to Snoodle's snuffling snout and Poppet's quick thinking, a candy cane found in the bottom of the cart and hurled at the next set of points sent the friends speeding after Katsuma again.

As they passed underneath a giant cake. Furi pulled out one of the sugar sticks holding the whole thing up.

'Oh, toffee apples!' Sweet Tooth screamed as the

cake crashed down onto the track. The Candy Cruiser was travelling too fast to stop in time. 'Aargh!' The villain's screams were abruptly cut-off as Sweet Tooth smashed into the cake's chocolate icing topping.

Katsuma grinned at the others as their carts came to a gentle stop at the end of the track. They were back in the jungle.

The friends sighed with relief – and then the carts abruptly tipped them out, dumping them in a pool of water as a sinister shadow glided past overhead.

High above the trees, *ScareForce One* soared majestically over the jungle in all its ominous glory, its engines thrumming.

'I've lost radio contact with Sweet Tooth,' explained Dr. Strangeglove, his sinister features visible on a large video screen inside the cockpit of *ScareForce One*, 'but Katsuma is still travelling with the furry buffoon, the pink poppety thing and the inconsequential snuffler.

My plan, however, is on track . . . as long as they collect the hatching ingredients . . . and you collect them.'

The evil genius's face loomed larger on the screen as he leant in towards the camera. 'Failure is not an option!'

Captain Pong gulped hard. It didn't do to upset Dr. Strangeglove.

Elsewhere aboard *ScareForce One*, Glump guards marched Luvli and Diavlo into secure cells. They could also hear Dr. Strangeglove's commands echoing from the airship's public address system.

The guards weren't taking any chances either. One of them put out Diavlo's smoking hot-top using a soda syphon, while another taped up Luvli's magical stalk.

'Watch the eyelashes, you beastly creature,' Luvli snarled at the Glumps.

'Still no sign of Zommer then,' Diavlo whispered to his friend and fellow prisoner.

Zommer was busy elsewhere, rocking out at the biggest gig of his career, playing for thousands of adoring Woolly Blue Hoodoos and Naughty Nutters back in the Hoodoo village.

As he came to the end of his set, rockets firing from his guitar, his name in flames behind him, the gigantic airship lumbered into view.

'Wait a minute! Wait a minute!' he shouted, lost in the moment. 'Let's do it one more time!'

But before he could, the pipe descended again and Zommer was sucked up from the stage. For a moment, silence fell across the village, and then a massive cheer went up from the crowd. It was the best show they had ever seen.

CHAPTER SEVENTEEN

Welcome to Jollywood!

Reaching the edge of the Gombala Gombala Jungle at last, Katsuma, Poppet, Furi, Mr. Snoodle and Blinki emerged from the green gloom beneath the trees and found themselves at the edge of the coast. The sound of waves crashing on the rocks at the foot of the cliffs rang in their ears.

Across the sea lay the mystical land of Jollywood. Furi sniffed. Spicy scents were in the air, while the twanging tones of distant sitars and the furious beeping of rickshaw horns carried to them on the sea-breeze.

Stretching across the sea, linking Music Island to

the mainland, was a broad bridge shaped like a gigantic piano keyboard. As the friends set off across the bridge, every key they stepped on played a different note.

'I hope the others are OK,' Poppet said, as the friends crossed the piano bridge. 'First Zommer, now Diavlo and Luvli. The way things are going there'll be none of us left.'

But Katsuma wasn't listening. He was more interested in showing off for Blinki, trying to play a tune as he hopped from key to key. 'Hi Yaa Hurricane!'

However, on the very last note he messed up, stomping on poor Mr. Snoodle instead. The Silly Snuffler gave a parp of surprise.

'Well here we are, Jollywood!' Katsuma announced, doing another piece to camera without even pausing to apologise to Mr. Snoodle. 'Let's go!' But the friends weren't going anywhere. Not just yet, anyway.

The bridge had brought them to a huge doorway set into a vast wall, beyond which lay the wonders of the mystical land of Jollywood.

'It's some kind of puzzle,' Poppet said, studying the strange markings on the door.

'Hey, leave this to me,' said Katsuma. It was time for the gooperstar to step up to the mark.

His paws flew over the symbols but the door remained stubbornly closed.

'I think a bit of brute Katsuma force might be in order.'

With a cry of 'Hi Yaa Hurrrrrricane!' Katsuma attempted his most difficult kung fu move yet as he tried to kick down the door. All he actually succeeded in doing was to hurt his foot. 'Ow-wow-wow-wow-wow-ow!'

As Katsuma sat on the ground nursing his poor toes, the door still closed, a local Jollywood shopkeeper carrying a heavy tray of food crossed the bridge behind the gang. The friends noticed now that set into the wall around the door were a series of mysterious Moshi glyphs. The shopkeeper punched a sequence of glyphs and the huge door groaned open, allowing the monster to walk straight through, taking his food with him.

The door slammed shut again behind the monster, as the gang stared on, gobsmacked. Poppet tried the handle, but the door remained stubbornly shut.

The aroma of spicy food hung in the air, soon finding its way up Furi's nose.

'Mmmmmm!' Furi purred. And in that moment, as the wonderful smell of the delicious delicacies worked their magic upon him, the big hairy brute had a brainwave.

'So the square root of a banana, multiplied by ten untangled pretzels,' he mused, peering at the glyphs through a pair of half-moon glasses, 'is equal to the chemical symbol for boron minus . . .'

'What does that mean?' Poppet butted in.

'It means I'm really hungry. So we push this then this then this.' As he spoke, Furi pushed several glyphs in sequence, and the door swung open once more.

Rushing off to scoff food from a tray another

Jollywood shopkeeper was carrying, Furi left Katsuma, Poppet, Snoodle and Blinki gazing about them in wonder. The marketplace they now found themselves in was a riot of sound and colour.

'So where are we gonna find a Blue Jeepers?' Katsuma asked 'And how are we going to get it to cry?'

Poppet gave him a look. 'Tell it one of your jokes?'

'Any idea where I can find a Blue Jeepers?' Katsuma asked a shopkeeper, pointedly ignoring Poppet's snide remark.

'Ringtanana beeener woah lala meena?' said the shopkeeper.

'Blue Jeepers? Moshling? Very rare?' Katsuma asked a random passer-by.

Poppet set off again, accompanied by Snoodle, her head back in the book. 'Left here, I think . . . right . . . ' – and bumped slap bang into a Moshling with a huge quiff of bright blue hair and wearing a sparkling white suit. His moustache was the same striking blue as his hair.

'Ooof! Er, who are you?' Poppet asked, surprised.

The Moshling bowed, bringing his palms together in greeting. 'I am Bobbi SingSong, international singing sensation and award-winning gooperstar of Jollywood stage and screen! My movies have been translated into over 400 languages!'

'A gooperstar, eh?' said Katsuma, wandering over. 'Not exactly A-list I'm guessing?'

Bobbi SingSong looked around furtively. 'I am travelling incognito.'

Katsuma stared at him blankly.

'Ah-ha!' the curious Moshling declared, quickly swapping his moustache for his monobrow, and vice versa.

Suddenly the marketplace went crazy as everyone instantly recognized the Jollywood gooperstar, though Katsuma couldn't see any difference in his appearance.

Bobbi SingSong was mobbed by a crowd of adoring fans, as a host of autograph books were thrust in his face. Katsuma looked on enviously.

'Bobbi! Bobbi! Bobbi!' the fans shrieked.

With a snap of his fingers, accompanied by the

screech of brakes and the smell of burning tyre rubber, a motorized rickshaw, blinged up to the max, pulled up in front of the Jollywood gooperstar.

A monster that looked like Bubba the bouncer from the Underground Disco in Monstro City, only wearing a turban, constructed a pile of spice crates so that Bobbi could climb onto the rickshaw's roof.

'Bobbi! Bobbi! Bobbi!' the crowd was chanting now.

'Calm down, there's plenty of Bobbi SingSong to go round!'

'Yeah, yeah. Plenty of Bobbi SingSong to go around,' Katsuma said cattily, doing a poor impersonation of the gooperstar.

'We were wondering, Mr SingSong,' Poppet shouted to be heard over the excitable crowd, 'do you know where we could find a Blue Jeepers? It's really important!'

'A Blue Jeepers?' Bobbi shouted back. 'I'm telling you, miss, they are rare. Very rare indeed! But I do know they love music and dancing! Then again, who doesn't?'

'Me!' muttered Katsuma.

'You know,' Bobbi went on, 'me personally, I find music can solve almost any problem!'

CHAPTER EIGHTEEN

What a Kerfuffle!

'*Welcome to Jollywood Jollywood jolly good Jollywood Jollywood*
Jollywood Jollywood jolly good Jollywood Jollywood
Jollywood Jollywood jolly good Jollywood Jollywood
Jollywood Jollywood jolly good Jollywood Jollywood.'

The Jollywood drums and sitar music began on cue as Bobbi SingSong and the crowd began to sing.

'Welcome, don't you dilly dally,
This might send you quite doolally,

Introducing a sensation,
Subject of great adulation.'

Led by the Jollywood Singaling, Katsuma, Poppet and Mr. Snoodle set off in search of the mysterious Blue Jeepers Moshling.

'See steamy jungles, explore mountains high,
Watch mystic gurus, sit back kiss the sky,
Go wiggle jingling bells on your wrist,
Pretzel yourself in a yoga-style twist.'

They found it meditating in a temple, high on a mountain, whilst levitating on a flying carpet. As soon as the friends appeared though, it vanished in a puff of smoke.

'I can make you move like Bobbi Bobbi SingSong,
(He can make you groove like Bobbi Bobbi SingSong.)
I can make you move like Bobbi Bobbi SingSong,
(He can make you groove like Bobbi Bobbi SingSong.)'

Returning to the bustling marketplace – where the Jollywood dance routine was in full swing now – Poppet spotted the sky-coloured Snuggly Tiger Cub riding an elephant. Katsuma, however, was starting to fall under the spell of the music. Much to his annoyance, his toes started to tap. Then his shoulders began to twitch.

> *'Head to the left then head to the right,*
> *Arms akimbo legs real tight.*
> *Fingers up and twitch your neck,*
> *Judder sideways hit the deck.*
> *One step here and one step there,*
> *Shake those hips and brush your h h h h h . . . '*

Meanwhile, Poppet and Snoodle were busy chasing the Blue Jeepers around the town, the Moshling having taken to the air on a small cloud as it played along with the music on a sitar.

> *'Jollywood Jollywood jolly good Jollywood Jollywood*
> *Jollywood Jollywood jolly good Jollywood Jollywood*

Jollywood Jollywood jolly good Jollywood Jollywood
Jollywood Jollywood jolly good Jollywood Jollywood.'

Catching sight of a snake charmer, Furi had an idea. It was the old Jollywood rope trick. Setting off up the snake charmer's rope, Furi got to the top only for the Blue Jeepers and his cloud to disappear again – a split second before the rope when slack . . .

> *'Head to the left then head to the right,*
> *Arms akimbo legs real tight.*
> *Fingers up and twitch your neck,*
> *Judder sideways hit the deck.*
> *One step here and one step there,*
> *Shake those hips and brush your h h h h h . . .*
> *It is jolly good in Jollywood!'*

A pair of curtains parted and Katsuma found himself gazing into the bright blue eyes of another Katsuma, just like him – only this one was wearing a veil and was of the female persuasion. As the infectious rhythms continued to work their magic, and his veiled friend's hips swayed in time to the music, Katsuma decided he liked dancing after all.

'Taking tea on my veranda,
Goodness me, things could not be grander.
I'm a Moshling with a mantra,
Errrr, I've forgotten what it is . . . it doesn't matter!'

Completely caught up in the music, Katsuma tried showing off to his new girlfriend. What started out as a Hi Yaa Hurricane kung fu move, ended up with him tripping over Mr. Snoodle again.

'Jollywood Jollywood jolly good Jollywood Jollywood
Jollywood Jollywood jolly good Jollywood Jollywood
Jollywood Jollywood jolly good Jollywood Jollywood
Jollywood Jollywood jolly good Jollywood Jollywood.'

The Snuggly Tiger Cub had seen the whole thing, and it was now laughing so much that tears of joy were streaming down its furry cheeks. With a helping trunk from a passing elephant, Poppet collected the tears in a glass vial and the second phase of their mission was complete! As suddenly as it had started, the song came to an end again and the crowd dispersed, street sellers going back to whatever it was they had been doing before Bobbi SingSong's performance had transformed the marketplace into a Jollywood extravaganza. The female Katsuma departed too, much to Katsuma's dismay.

'See, what did I tell you?' Bobbi said, signing a few last autographs as Poppet put a stopper in the vial of Blue Jeepers' tears she had collected and popped it into Strangeglove's briefcase. 'A good old Jollywood extravaganza solves any problem.'

'Thanks, Mr SingSong,' Poppet replied, 'but I doubt even you could solve our next challenge. Isn't that right, Katsuma?'

But Katsuma was now busy talking to Blinki. 'Look I'm not asking you, I'm telling you. Delete that bit where I made a fool of myself.'

Blinki whispered something in Katsuma's ear.

'Whaddya mean, which one?'

'Katsuma?'

'What, oh yeah,' Katsuma said, acknowledging Poppet at last and picking up the suitcase. 'We need to find the mythical Frosted Rainbow Rox. But the journal says it's halfway up Sillimanjaroooooooh!'

Katsuma's arm began to shake as the briefcase lit up again. Strangeglove's face peered at them from the built-in TV screen.

'Against all odds you have successfully collected item number two! But remember you'll need all three artefacts to win Strangeglove's eggy challenge! Mwa-ha!' Strangeglove's tone changed from that of cheesy game show host to evil megalomaniac again. 'Tick tock, tick tock,' he said, holding up the poor unfortunate Mini Ben out front of him. 'Better hurry!'

'Why that jumped up, moustachioed . . .' Katsuma fumed as the suitcase returned to normal.

'If you are in a hurry, why don't you just kerfuffle yourselves?' Bobbi SingSong suggested.

'Ker-whattle ourselves?' the gang asked as one.

'Kerfuffle yourselves. It's the only way to travel. Now then, please be getting in a huddle.' The gang looked at each other, as confused as a bewildered Batty Bubblefish. 'Come along, it's easy!'

Furi, Katsuma and Poppet huddled together, Katsuma grasping the briefcase tightly while Poppet held one of Snoodle's little paws and Furi another.

'Now close your eyes . . . think of where you are wanting to go. And most important, please do not be breaking the circle!'

Bobbi began to sing again, accompanied by the Blue Jeepers on the sitar.

'Just close your eyes and kerfuffle,' the Jollywood sensation sang, performing a weird yoga move as he did so. 'Just close your eyes and relax, just close your eyes and kerfuffle, and you'll be making tracks.'

Stars began to swirl around the monsters' heads, just as another shopkeeper carrying another tray of delicious food passed by. Furi opened his eyes, captivated by the wonderful aroma rather than Bobbi SingSong's swami moves.

And then – *Poof!* – the huddle of monsters vanished.

'Rrrrrrr!' Bobbi sighed. 'What a kerfuffle!'

CHAPTER NINTEEN

The Snows of Sillimanjaro

The foothills of Sillimanjaro were blanketed in snow, a freezing gale sending ice flakes whirling into the air and obscuring the view of the mountain beyond. The landscape was as white and as cold as a Wistful Snowtot's nose.

With a Poof! Katsuma, Poppet and Mr. Snoodle materialised in the middle of the blizzard.

Snoodle and Katsuma looked at one another – one standing on top of the other – clutching at their arms and bodies, hardly able to believe that they were still in one piece.

'Are you OK?' Katsuma asked.

'I think so,' Poppet said, pinching herself.

Katsuma shivered. 'Remind me to kerfuffle first class next time.'

Snoodle jumped down into the snow. Poppet looked round. 'Hey, where's Furi?'

Somewhere else nowhere near Mount Sillimanjaro, Furi suddenly appeared inside a conveniently empty cell aboard *ScareForce One*. Peering between the bars of the cell next to him he saw Luvli and Diavlo, who looked back at him, stunned.

'Er, got anything to eat?' the always hungry monster asked.

In the frozen foothills of Sillimanjaro Poppet said, 'He must have kerfuffled somewhere else!'

'Hey!' Katsuma exclaimed, seized by panic.

'Where's Blinki?'

'Oh no! Not Blinki, too!'

'We can't make an award-winning action/adventure docudrama that will be nominated in six categories including best leading actor without Blinki!' Katsuma was in despair. How was he ever going to become the gooperstar he deserved to be, if the Moshling-cam wasn't there to record his brave, heart-rending performance?

'Look.' Poppet was pointing at Mr. Snoodle, who was busy snuffling about in the snow. 'Snoodle's picked up a scent.'

The Moshling started to dig.

'He's found him!' Katsuma exclaimed excitedly, as the Silly Snuffler exposed first a dully blinking antenna and then a large glassy, camera-lens eye.

Blinki was frozen solid, as cold as an Abominable Snowling. His eyelid quivered.

'C'mon Blinki, you can make it,' Katsuma encouraged his friend. 'You're the only Moshicam we've got!'

With a loud doing! a spring sprung out of the All-Seeing Moment Muncher's camera casing. Katsuma slumped down in the snow, thoroughly fed up. 'Great, now how are we going to film me saving the day?'

Poppet turned on him at that, her pink-furred face red with rage. 'It's not about you! It's about rescuing the Great Moshling Egg. C'mon, we've got a Frosted Rainbow Rox to find!'

The wind was starting to pick up.

'And fast, there's a storm coming!'

'You're right,' Katsuma agreed reluctantly, and then added a half-hearted, 'Hi Yaa hurricane . . .'

He attempted his kung fu move, but his heart wasn't in that either. Poppet was too busy wrapping the frozen Moment Muncher in a cloth to notice. Having done that, she put Blinki carefully inside her rucksack.

Back aboard *ScareForce One*, Diavlo, Furi and Luvli were discussing their plight, the three of them having been locked up in cells next to each other.

'I'm telling you, Bumblechops was right,' Diavlo said. 'Something big is going down. I mean humongous. We're talking end of the world stuff here.'

'It did sound rather ghastly,' Luvli agreed.

Furi looked from one to the other, an anxious expression on his face. 'Yeah, let's just hope Katsuma can grab that egg. Mmmm, egg . . . ' he said dreamily. 'Fried? Boiled? Scrambled? Poached? Devilled?'

ScareForce One slowly drifted on its way disappearing into a bank of cloud.

'Oeufs en cocotte a la crème . . . '

Halfway up Mount Sillimanjaro a blizzard was raging. Katsuma and Poppet trudged on through deep snow up to their waists, which meant that Mr. Snoodle was forced to follow in their footsteps, or be buried altogether.

Poppet was still studying Furbert Snufflepeeps'

journal even though she was in a virtual white-out.

'This is crazy,' Katsuma shouted to be heard over the howling gale, 'we'll never find the Frosted Rainbow Rox in this blizzard!'

Poppet whispered in the yellow Snuffler's ear. 'C'mon, Snoodle, how's about some snuffling?'

Snoodle looked thoroughly miserable, icicles hanging from the end of his nose. He wasn't his usual healthy sunshine yellow colour any more either. He was starting to go blue from the cold.

'Oh no, Snoodle's a bluedle!' Poppet moped. 'He can't handle this cold.'

Picking him up, she placed the Silly Snuffler inside her backpack too.

'He's not the only one!' complained Katsuma. He was shivering too, now, hugging his arms to his body against the cold.

The storm was getting worse.

'Look, a cave. Let's go there 'til the storm passes!'

'But what about Monstro City?' Poppet asked,

watching as Katsuma headed off through the whirling snow.

'What about it? In case you hadn't noticed, **WE'RE IN THE MIDDLE OF A BLIZZARD!**'

'Katsuma! Don't shout!' Poppet called, trying not to shout herself, but desperately keen to get Katsuma to quieten down.

Katsuma put his hands around his mouth to make himself heard over the howling gale. 'Why? You think I'm gonna **TRIGGER AN AVALAAANCHE?**' he shouted. And promptly triggered an avalanche.

CHAPTER TWENTY

Snow Joke

'You OK?' Katsuma's concerned voice echoed from the walls of the ice cave into which he had dragged the friends in order to escape the avalanche.

Shivering and completely blue now, Mr. Snoodle looked like he was on his last legs. Katsuma was vainly attempting to set fire to a pile of twigs using a pair of flints.

'No!' Poppet wailed, close to tears. 'If we don't get out of here soon Mr. Snoodle's not going to make it!'

'And Blinki?'

Poppet peered inside her backpack. 'He needs defrosting, fast!'

Katsuma tried the flints again. This time a spark sprang from the stones and set fire to the twigs. Katsuma jumped for joy.

The snuffling Mr. Snoodle sneezed, and blew out the flame.

'Ah, I'm sorry,' Katsuma moaned, 'I guess it's kind of my fault.'

'It's all your fault.' Poppet started to cry.

Katsuma stared at his friend. That wasn't quite the reaction he had been expecting. Things really were as bad as they seemed. When they had set out on their mission to recover the three artefacts it had all seemed like an awesome adventure. Now, trapped in a frozen cave with his friends in danger and no chance of a rescue, the situation looked bleak. Unable to help himself, he burst into tears. 'I never thought it would be like this!' he sobbed.

'Come on, Katsuma,' Poppet sniffed, regaining her composure. 'There's always hope!'

'Nah, not this time. I've ruined everything.'

'Hey, when did your get up and go get up and leave?' Poppet challenged him. 'I didn't have you down as a pessimist.'

'I'm not, I just think awful things are going to happen!'

Katsuma put his head in his paws in despair. Poppet had never seen him so genuinely upset. So vulnerable.

She began to sing.

'When you've lost all your sunshine, hope can throw you a lifeline. Friends will help through the darkness.'

One tiny twig on the campfire was still glowing. Poppet bent down and blew on its gently, coaxing it into life, and the fire began to ignite.

'We can do it, yes we can do it.'

'No we can't,' muttered Katsuma.

'We pull together then there's really nothing to it.'

'Forget it.'

'Oh we can do it, yes, we can do it. Look inside your heart, just make a start and we'll get through it. Yeah, we can do it.'

'No we can't!' Katsuma protested.

'But we gotta get to it.'

'Not a chance!'

'If we're together then we'll never be alone. When thoughts are little seeds, make sure they're flowers not weeds.'

'I can't do it!'

'With this philosophy, don't give in and we'll win – you and me!'

'I don't think so, we're in a proper jam,' Katsuma began to sing, Poppet accompanying him with a few choice la-la-las. *'Maybe we can. Sounds like a plan. I see some silver lining.'* The magic of the song had taken a hold of Katsuma's flagging spirits at last.

'We can do it!' Poppet cheered him on.

'I feel like hope's thrown us a rope. Maybe we'll . . .'

'*. . . Turn things round,*' the two friends sang in

unison. *'When clouds creep in, that's OK. Just shoo them right away! When things go wrong, and they will, buckle up, sing this song . . . '*

'. . . Climb that hill!' cheered Poppet.

'We can do it' – now it was Katsuma's turn – *'I always said we could!'*

'You misunderstood!' sang a flower that popped out of the ground as the fire grew hotter and the ice began to melt.

And it wasn't only flowers that were appearing from the ice. A long frozen Valiant Viking defrosted, shaking himself dry like a wet dog as he woke up from his ice age-long hibernation.

> *'Oh we can do it,*
> *Yes we can do it,*
> *If we pull together then there's really nothing to it!*
> *Yeah we can do it,*
> *Yes we can do it,*

*Look inside your heart just make a start and we'll get
through it.
Yeah we can do it, but we gotta get to it,
If we're together then there's really nothin' to it.
Oh we can do it,
Yes we can do it,
And we'll beat all the odds for sure!
We can do it!'*

Warmed by the crackling fire, soon Snoodle and Blinki
were feeling toasty. As the icicles – and even the cave! –
melted away, blue skies were revealed above.

The melting ice revealed the entrance to a tunnel
that glittered and sparkled with multi-coloured light.
Taking a burning branch for a torch, Katsuma led
the way, as the friends excitedly followed the tunnel
to another cavern. Rainbow light reflected from the
glistening walls of the cave, making the monsters gasp
in amazement.

The spectrum beams were coming from the centre of the cave, and a glittering treasure, the like of which not one of them had ever seen before. It couldn't be anything else . . . it had to be the Frosted Rainbow Rox that they had been searching for all this time.

'We did it!' Poppet cheered. 'All three artefacts!'

Holding the torch close to the block of ice containing their prize, Katsuma watched in excited anticipation as the ice there melted too and the marvellous Frosted Rainbow Rox was revealed at last. Katsuma picked it up reverently in both hands and placed it carefully inside the briefcase. The last space had been filled.

He wasn't surprised when the briefcase lit up this time and Strangeglove's face appeared once more on the built-in TV screen.

'Is that your final artefact?' the villain's voice buzzed from the briefcase. 'Are you sure? Are you confident? Are you . . .'

'Yes, we know,' said Poppet, slamming the case

shut, cutting him off, 'tick tock, tick tock.'

Grabbing Katsuma by the arm she dragged him towards the cave entrance.

'Let's get out of here!'

CHAPTER
TWENTY-ONE

A Meeting of Minds

Reaching the peak of Mount Sillimanjaro at last, Poppet and Katsuma climbed the icy stairs to the entrance of the abandoned cable car station.

The place was deserted. Their footsteps echoed from the silent winding mechanism and disused cable cars, their breath frosting on the freezing air.

'Hello? Hello? Show yourself, Strangeglove. We've got your precious artefacts!'

Katsuma looked at Poppet. Poppet was looking nervous.

'Can you believe it? We go through all this and he doesn't even . . .'

'Show up?' Katsuma fell silent as maniacal laughter echoed around the empty station. 'Mwa-haha! I might be the most mendacious villain Monstro City has ever seen but I'm never late.'

Strangeglove and his sidekick emerged from the shadows. They were pushing a trolley before them. Katsuma gasped. Lying on the trolley was the Great Moshling Egg.

'Dr. Strangeglove, I presume!' declared Poppet.

Katsuma looked the megalomaniac mastermind up and down. 'You look much taller on TV.'

'Oh you think so? Yes, I get that a lot but they say . . .' Strangeglove caught himself. 'Enough of this asinine banter! I assume you have my artefacts? I'd hate to be forced to pulverise such a precious chooky eggy.' His gloved hand hovered over the egg, bunched into a fist.

'Quit twisting our gooberries. We've got 'em.'

Katsuma walked to the centre of the room and

opened the case, revealing the three artefacts lying inside.

'Fishlips, confirm their authenticity!' Strangeglove commanded.

Fishlips bounced over to the case. Taking out a strange gizmo, he scanned the three artefacts, the wand bleeping as he passed it over the contents of the case.

'All hunky dory here, boss!'

Strangeglove rubbed his hands together with glee. 'Hahaa! At last I can concoct my hatching ser . . . um, enjoy these ultra-rare goodies!'

Katsuma and Poppet gave each other a look as the doctor stopped himself, just before he gave the game away. But it was enough. Buster Bumblechops had been right – Strangeglove did indeed intend to hatch the egg.

'Just hand over the egg and we'll be on our way,' Katsuma said, trying to sound calm.

'You know the drill,' countered Strangeglove. 'First you hand me the case.'

'The egg!' Poppet said forcefully, a bead of sweat

creeping down the side of her face.

'The case!' Strangeglove declared not backing down.

'The egg!' Poppet insisted.

'The case!' persisted the doctor.

'The egg!'

'Case!'

'Egg!'

'Case!'

Fishlips' gaze flipped from Strangeglove to Poppet and back again.

'Egg!'

'Case!'

'Hey, this is like ping pong!' Fishlips gawped, transfixed.

'Case!'

Strangeglove gave a bark of cruel laughter as he whipped a remote control from the pocket of his coat and pressed a button. The briefcase immediately sprouted legs.

'Uh . . . OK . . . ' Katsuma said uncertainly as the

briefcase strolled across the room, joining the doctor on the other side. 'Now hand over the egg!'

'Haha! Poor deluded fools. Did you really think I'd hand the Great Moshling Egg over to a pair of, of . . . Moshi Monsters?'

Strangeglove snapped his fingers and suddenly Glumps appeared from every part of the cable car station, where moments before there had been none.

'Glumps!' the doctor said, as his army of transformed Moshlings gathered round him. 'Go do that goodoo that you do so well. Mwahahaha!'

Without another word the Glumps began to close in on the friends.

Katsuma froze, taken aback by the sudden appearance of the Glumps. And then, in the next moment, he pulled himself together and sprang into action.

'Poppet!' he shouted. 'The seeds!'

Poppet didn't need telling twice. She pulled out a packet of Moshling seeds and threw them at the advancing Glumps. The packet opened and the seeds spilled out, rolling across the floor of the cable car station like so many marbles.

The effect on the Glumps was the same as if they had been marbles. Strangeglove's minions slipped on the seeds, spinning and tumbling out of control.

Katsuma launched himself into the air with a bound, performing a series of impressive moves – all whilst still in mid-air – taking out the Glumps that stood in his way. Grabbing hold of a dangling rope he swung past the trolley, grabbing the egg as he did so.

'Stop them, you fools!' Strangeglove cried as Katsuma spun through the air, egg in hand.

Poppet was delighted. 'We got it. Let's get outta here!'

'No!' Strangeglove seethed.

Something suddenly caught the master villain's eye. It was a blinking red light poking out of the top of Poppet's backpack.

Blinki was fully operational again and, as the doctor watched, the All-Seeing Moment Muncher floated out of the pack into the air. His 'record' light was on.

'Look, look!' Strangeglove called to Katsuma. 'Your audience is ready for your close up!'

'Blinki!' Katsuma gasped in delight.

'Katsuma, no!' Poppet yelled, wise to Strangeglove's mind games.

'Now watch this,' Katsuma called. 'Hi Yaa Hurricane!'

He just couldn't help himself. He had to pull off just a few more fancy moves for the benefit of Blinki and his imagined audience.

Only he couldn't help messing up either.

Fumbling the precious egg, Katsuma fell forward. The Great Moshling Egg went flying from his hands.

Fishlips lined up the trolley. As the egg landed back in the trolley, Katsuma landed on top of Poppet, the two of them tumbling into a pile of snow in an undignified heap.

'Narcissistic numbskull!' Strangeglove laughed and pressed another button on the remote control. 'Going down!'

With a grinding of rusted gears and the screech of unoiled cables taking up the tension, the cable car station came to life. Cogs whirred, sirens blared and the nearest cable car started to move.

Katsuma and Poppet looked at each other. 'Huh?'

Strangeglove strolled over to the cable car, briefcase in hand.

'Well you didn't think I'd arrange a mountain top rendezvous without organising a dramatic exit, did you? TTFN!'

'See ya, wouldn't wanna be ya!' Fishlips chanted.

Poppet and Katsuma watched helplessly, still tangled in a heap on the floor, as Strangeglove, Fishlips and the mob of Glumps boarded the cable car.

And then suddenly, Mr. Snoodle appeared from where he had been hiding and he was hopping mad. 'Grrr!' the Silly Snuffler snarled.

Before Poppet could grab him, Mr. Snoodle made a mad leap for the cable car as it set off down the mountainside.

CHAPTER TWENTY-TWO

On the Edge

'Mr. Snoodle, noooooo!' Poppet's cry echoed from the walls of the cable car station as the Silly Snuffler landed on the roof of Strangeglove's carriage.

The machinery continued to grind as the cable car headed down the mountain.

'Katsuma! We've got to stop them!'

Katsuma frantically looked around the station. And then his eyes fell on something, something that was perfect for the job. Picking up the pair of old skis, he hurled them between the crunching cogs of the winding mechanism.

Halfway down the side of the mountain, the cable car jerked to a halt with a painful mechanical squeal and was left swinging over a vast expanse of nothingness.

'Come on!' Poppet shouted, running out onto the station balcony.

Katsuma and Blinki followed, chasing after the pink-furred monster as she raced towards a tourist telescope, positioned at the edge of the peak.

Poppet peered through the eyepiece. She saw the cable car swinging violently over the perilous drop beneath it.

Refocusing the telescope, she peered through a window and into the swaying gondola itself.

Inside the cable car it was total chaos. There were Glumps everywhere. They were struggling to keep Mr. Snoodle at bay as he scurried around them, trying to get at the egg.

'Begone, you doodling snuffler!' Strangeglove raged,

swiping at Snoodle with his cane. 'Fishlips, do . . . something. Anything!'

'Sure,' Fishlips said, pulling out a comb and paper kazoo, 'you hum it and I'll play it!'

'Mindless moron!'

Grabbing hold of Snoodle, Strangeglove threw the furious Moshling off him, the Silly Snuffler landing on a trapdoor in the floor of the carriage. Picking up Fishlips, the doctor hurled his sidekick at a lever, which caused the trapdoor to swing open.

For a moment it looked like Mr. Snoodle might fall through it, until he managed to grab hold of the edge of the door by his paws.

'Snoodle! Be careful!' Poppet wailed, still watching through the telescope. The Moshling's hind legs were dangling out of the bottom of the cable car.

Strangeglove bore down on the struggling Silly Snuffler. 'And so, my meddling Moshling, prepare to take one giant leap for Moshikind.'

Strangeglove brought his foot down hard, attempting

to crush Snoodle's paw beneath his heel.

Snoodle pulled his paw out of the way just in time, but now he was left hanging on to the lip of the trapdoor by just one paw.

Strangeglove turned to Fishlips. 'Remember when I said, deep down, I was a good guy?'

'Er . . . ' Fishlips replied, uncertainly.

'I lied!'

Dr. Strangeglove brought his foot down again. With a pained 'Honk!' the Silly Snuffler flinched and let go, falling from the cable car and plummeting into the abyss.

CHAPTER TWENTY-THREE

Doomed!

'N**ooooooooooo!**' Poppet turned away from the telescope and put her head in her paws.

Katsuma looked at her, distraught. He moved to comfort her, not knowing what else to do, but Poppet only shrugged him away. They were beaten. Dr. Strangeglove had won.

Blinki looked up anxiously as a vast shadow moved across the platform of the mountain viewpoint and *ScareForce One* hovered into view above them.

'Run!' shouted Katsuma as he caught sight of the approaching airship. Grabbing Poppet by the hand, the two of them turned and headed for the station again. They hadn't got very far when the snaking suction hose was lowered from the blimp and sucked them up – Blinki included.

ScareForce One turned, heading towards the cable car. A rope was lowered from its gondola, enabling Strangeglove, Fishlips and the other Glumps to grab hold.

'Captain Pong! To my lair!' Strangeglove commanded, still clutching the egg and the briefcase, as *ScareForce One* took off towards the horizon. 'Mwahahaaaa!' the doctor laughed in triumph. 'HA HA. MWA HAA.'

His laughter was infectious. 'Haahaaaa!' Fishlips joined in.

The Moshi Monsters had been defeated, their quest ultimately ending in failure. Dr. Strangeglove had captured them all and they were now all locked up together in a cage at the heart of the villain's underground lair.

Poppet was singing sorrowfully as she stared at a picture of herself and her favourite Moshling in happier times. 'Now he's gone. Mr. Snoodle.'

Katsuma was silent.

Luvli moved to comfort her tearful friend. 'Maybe he's in a better place.'

'A burger joint?' suggested Furi.

'He never hurt anyone,' Diavlo fumed. 'It makes me so MAD!'

He was so mad, flames started to crackle from the top of his head.

At that moment, Strangeglove entered the chamber on an articulated platform, his sidekick Fishlips at his side.

'Well, well, well,' the doctor gloated. 'Isn't this a jolly little soiree?'

'You beast!' Poppet screamed. 'You pompous, cowardly . . .'

'Please, spare me the compliments,' the doctor interrupted her, 'and let's get down to business.'

'Er, boss, I don't think she meant . . . '

Taking hold of his cane as if it was a golf club, Strangeglove teed up and with one thwack walloped Fishlips away across the room.

'The time has come,' the villainous mastermind taunted the friends. 'Soon I will Glump the mighty critter inside the Great Moshling Egg . . . using the ingredients YOU so kindly collected for me! Mwaha!'

'Big surprise!' Poppet was still upset but Strangeglove's gloating had brought out her feisty side. 'You think we didn't know that all along? We had everything planned but . . . ' Poppet glanced at Katsuma, but he was still staring vacantly into space, managing to look both embarrassed and downhearted at the same time. 'But, things just didn't pan out,' she said, crestfallen.

'You won't get away with this!' Diavlo bellowed, blowing his top.

'Oh really? Who's going to stop me, hothead? You? Haha!'

Whipping out his throat spray dispenser, Strangeglove turned it on Diavlo, extinguishing the fiery monster's smoking crater. The triumphant villain rode the platform to the top of his monstrous Glumping machine, which was now in full swing.

ShiShi the Sneezing Panda was cowering in the glass holding chamber at the top of the contraption along with a host of other Moshlings.

'Help me' – ShiShi sneezed – 'please!'

'Help? Of course, ikkle ShiShi,' Strangeglove teased the terrified beastie, 'seeing as you said pwease!'

He flicked a switch, and the glumping process began. ShiShi was sucked into a tube and sent hurtling on its way into the heart of the Glumpatron 9000.

'And to think I could release these pathetic Moshlings with the secret melody that opens my Cloncotronic musical lock.'

'You mean the one that goes . . . ' Fishlips blew a raspberry riff of Dr. Strangeglove's self-penned theme tune.

'Ignoramus!' Strangeglove roared, planting his cane in Fishlips' mouth before he could finish and give away the last note. 'Now come along, there's hatching and glumping to be done!' he said, regaining control of his emotions, before adding for the Moshis' benefit, 'I'm sure you'll find it a moving experience.'

He flicked another switch on the control panel in front of him and the startled monsters felt a jolt as their cage began to move.

'What the . . . ?' Katsuma exclaimed.

The cage was being transported along a conveyor belt.

'Prepare to meet your doom!'

At the end of the conveyor was a doorway that led to a monstrous mashing machine. A sign hanging from the machine read: 'Your Doom'.

As the monsters struggled with their bonds, the clanking conveyor belt continued to carry the cage closer and closer to the machine. Strangeglove and Fishlips left the chamber without a second thought.

CHAPTER TWENTY-FOUR

Glumpity Glumpity Glump

I ts engines thrumming, *ScareForce One* reached its ultimate destination, hovering over the vast, foot-shaped valley. A hatch opened in the middle of the footprint and Strangeglove and Fishlips emerged, still aboard their ascending platform.

Strangeglove was looking like even more of a fashion disaster than usual, wearing weird wizardy robes. The crazed doctor held the Great Moshling Egg before him in both hands.

A host of Glumps was gathered around the platform. An army.

Blinki the All-Seeing Moment Muncher was clamped inside a restraining device and being forced to film the proceedings.

As his nefarious scheme reached its climax – syringe-tipped hoses snaking towards the egg – Strangeglove was clearly starting to enjoy himself. *'Glumpity glumpity glump glump! La dee dee! Glumpity glumpity!'* he sang.

Beneath the valley, in Strangeglove's lair, the Glumpatron 9000 was still glumping away noisily as the Moshis edged ever closer to their doom. But they weren't done yet. They weren't going down without a fight!

'It's no use, man!' Zommer groaned, pushing on the door at the top of the cage, a door which remained stubbornly locked.

'I'm sorry, guys,' Katsuma apologized for the umpteenth time. 'If I hadn't messed up my Hi Yaa Hurricane . . . '

'I, I, I!' Poppet yelled. 'For the last time, this isn't

about you! It never was! Thanks to your showboating Strangeglove's got the egg and Mr. Snoodle is . . . is gone!'

'I don't know what else to say,' Katsuma said, as Poppet burst into tears. 'I, we . . . '

'Say nothing! Just think of a way to get us outta here, fast! We need to get to that musical lock and save these Moshlings!'

Working together, the Moshis all strained at the cage but the door still wouldn't budge.

Diavlo's rage was bubbling to the surface again. 'When I get my hands on that . . . '

'Shhh . . . ' Poppet said, perking up.

'What is it?' Katsuma asked.

'Nothing, I thought I heard . . . it's nothing.'

Katsuma's ears pricked up as from far off in the distance there came a faint parping sound. 'No wait, I can hear it too!'

'Hey look, over there!' Diavlo pointed. A pair of yellow paws poked out of a vent in the air conditioning system.

'Hey, it's Mr. Snoodle! He's alive!' Poppet thrilled. 'Mr. Snoodle! Mr. Snoodle!'

With a loud clang, the vent fell open and the Silly Snuffler appeared. Mr. Snoodle jumped down onto the cage and unlatched the door with the flick of a paw.

'Oh, Snoodle, I thought you were gone forever!' Poppet gasped as the friends all climbed out onto the top of the cage.

'I don't understand,' Katsuma said, both pleased and relieved in equal measure. 'How did you . . . ?'

Snoodle parped softly in Poppet's ear and told her what had happened.

Once Snoodle had let go of the cable car and plummeted into the abyss, the wind began to whistle through his snout like a kettle coming to the boil.

Realizing what was happening, Snoodle smiled and the kettle noise gradually became a much more tuneful whistling.

It was joined by the waka-waka of rotor blades as a flock of Twirly Tiddlycopters came into view having heard Snoodle's whistle.

Poppet squeezed Snoodle hard. 'Wow! Whistling really does work!'

'I hate to break up such a beautiful reunion,' Luvli said, breaking up just such a beautiful reunion, 'but do you think you could speed it up?'

The friends were about to meet their doom. There was no time to lose. They leapt from the top of the cage, a split second before it bashed through the doors to be smashed to smithereens by the mashing machine on the other side.

In the footprint crater, Dr. Strangeglove was in full swing and revelling in the moment. His concoction was complete. The egg started to judder.

'And now the moment you've all been waiting for,' – the moment Strangeglove had been waiting for, anyway – 'Endlethon lavender othian. Mmblap, squiddle, roodleplap and . . .'

In Strangeglove's lair below, the Moshis were standing before the wheezing and parping Glumpatron 9000.

'It's too high!' Poppet peered up at the holding bulb of the Glumping machine. 'How're we gonna get up there to free the Moshlings? Luvli, how about some of your magic?' she said, brightening.

Luvli screwed up her face in concentration and her magical stalk began to quiver and glow. But then, despite her best efforts, the glow faded and the stalk flopped down again.

'It's no good, darling. I'm too pooped for any hokery pokery.'

'I can't get any higher!' Diavlo strained, trying to fly up to the imprisoned Moshlings but the ball and chain locked around his leg was holding him down.

'Higher? Hi yaa!' Poppet exclaimed, as an idea struck her. 'That's it! Katsuma, you can save the day after all!'

'I can? I mean, I can!' Katsuma said with growing confidence. 'How?'

'You can get up there using your Hi Yaa Hurricane!'

'Uh, well yeah, maybe.' Katsuma didn't sound so sure. 'But there's no way I can open that musical lock.'

'Sure you can! Just whistle the tune.' Poppet whistled the same tune she had heard Fishlips whistling – the one Strangeglove had stopped his sidekick whistling before he gave the game away. 'Or something like that . . . '

Katsuma turned his back on the others and putting his lips together, tried his best to whistle. But it was just as bad as before. Going blue in the face, all that escaped his lips were raspberries and spit!

'Katsuma?'

'I . . . ' This was the moment Katsuma had been

dreading, the moment he had to confess all to his friends. The moment he would let them down like never before . . . 'I can't whistle,' he said simply, his shoulders sagging.

'Ha ha. Very funny.' Poppet didn't sound in the least bit amused.

'Like, quit fooling around dude,' Zommer joined in.

'No, really, I can't! See?' He tried again, to prove a point, and succeeded; he couldn't whistle a single note. 'Don't ask me why.'

'Why?' asked Furi.

'I'm sorry. I guess . . . I guess I'm just not cut out to be the greatest hero that ever lived.' Katsuma slumped to the ground and lay on the floor in despair.

As the others stared at him, shell-shocked, Mr. Snoodle trotted over to the orange monster and started whistling in his ear. There was something familiar about the tune, something about it that stirred Katsuma into action again. It was the 'We can do it' song Poppet had sung in the ice cave on Mount Sillimanjaro.

'That's it, Snoodle! You're right! We can do it. You and me!' Katsuma grabbed hold of Snoodle and, holding him tight, said, 'Ready?'

Snoodle nodded.

'Hi Yaaaa!' Katsuma screeched, making his move. Bouncing off walls and somersaulting through the air, he landed on top of the platform, high above the floor of the chamber, where the musical lock was located. Thrusting Snoodle towards the lock he said, 'Over to you, Snoodle!'

Taking a deep breath, the Silly Snuffler whistled into the lock.

A number of lights lit up around the door to the holding chamber but one remained stubbornly red. Snoodle tried again, but still the last light refused to change colour. Snoodle didn't know all the notes to the tune – but someone did.

From inside the Glumpatron 9000 Stanley the Songful SeaHorse tooted the final note. A smile spreading across his face, Mr. Snoodle tried one last time. This time, the light changed from red to green and the door to the containment chamber opened.

Snoodle and Katsuma threw their arms around each other in a huge hug. All the Moshlings were safe.

A cheer rose from the rest of the gang below. Katsuma and Snoodle had done it – together!

'It's time we paid the doctor a visit!' Katsuma declared, striking a pose. 'Hi Yaaaa!'

CHAPTER
TWENTY-FIVE

Tables are Turned

Back inside the giant foot crater, Fishlips watched in awe as a podium rose out of the ground in front of Dr. Strangeglove. A large button stood proud of the pedestal – a button that would complete the process and inject the Great Moshling Egg with Strangeglove's foul concoction.

'Can I press the button, boss?' Fishlips enquired excitedly.

'Yes, Fishlips, you can press the button, but you may not!' Strangeglove raised both his hands into the air above the pedestal. 'It's Glumpageddon Time!'

But in his moment of glory, the megalomaniacal genius faltered as his words were interrupted by a distant parping sound.

'Who dares . . . ' he began, and then he caught sight of a bright yellow figure high up on a ridge at the edge of the gigantic footprint. The Silly Snuffler was tooting away bravely, a flag held in his paws.

At sight of the brave little Moshling, Strangeglove was overcome by uncontrollable laughter.

'Mwa ha . . . mwah . . . ha . . . mwahahahahahaha! Aw look!' he said putting on a mocking baby voice again. 'The bwave likkle Snuffler lives! How adowable! He finks he's gonna defeat the doctor!'

The Glump army joined their maniacal master in his mocking laughter then.

'You and whose army?' Strangeglove roared.

ShiShi the Sneezing Panda appeared at Mr. Snoodle's side.

'Oh haha!' Strangeglove laughed on. 'This is too delicious for words! I . . . '

Then Mini Ben appeared alongside Snoodle and ShiShi.

'Hold on, how did they . . . '

The doctor was shocked into silence as Katsuma, Poppet, Zommer, Furi, Luvli and Diavlo all appeared on top of the hill beside the Moshlings.

'Erm, Doc, I have a bad feeling about this . . . ' Fishlips muttered. The whole length of the ridge was filled with angry Moshlings. Hundreds . . . no . . . thousands of them!

'On Mr. Snoodle's signal,' Katsuma commanded, 'unleash . . . Moshlings!'

'Parp!' trumpeted Mr. Snoodle, and the Moshling horde charged down the slope towards the platform, the Glumps and the dastardly doctor.

'Fishlips, I . . . Fishlips?'

Strangeglove looked about him in a panic, as Twirly Tiddlycopters and a host of other flying Moshlings swooped down out of the sky, and his sidekick turned tail and fled.

'Fishlips! Wait, help me, nooo!'

Fearing for his own safety, Strangeglove turned on

his heel and ran – but not before he hit the button to complete the process that would transform the egg into the most monstrous Glump Moshi world had ever seen.

It was now or never. Mr. Snoodle launched himself into the air, knocking the egg clear as the injectors expelled their disgusting contents. But rather than entering the egg the muck splattered harmlessly over the platform.

Katsuma and Poppet watched as Snoodle and the egg tumbled through the air before they came back down to earth, the Silly Snuffler landing in Poppet's arms while Katsuma deftly caught the egg.

As the battle raged on inside the crater, *ScareForce One* started to turn, its captain clearly intending to flee too. As it did so, a squadron of Tiddlycopters turned on the airship.

'Abandon ship!' Captain Pong's voice carried over the crater, as the airship limped away, trailing smoke.

As the Glumps fled, where before there had been nothing but an army of Dr. Strangeglove's minions, now there was a sea of Moshlings, the Great Moshling Egg raised high above their heads.

Amidst all the mayhem and joyous celebrations, Katsuma turned to Poppet, gesturing so that all the victorious monsters and Moshlings could see.

'We did it!' he cheered, joining Poppet, Furi, Luvli, Diavlo and Zommer in an almighty celebratory group hug, as Blinki hovered above them, filming the triumphant heroes.

CHAPTER
TWENTY-SIX

Party Time

A heroes' welcome awaited the Moshis when they arrived in Monstro City. Monsters and Moshlings of all kinds fell into step behind them as the friends rock 'n' rolled along Main Street, heading towards Buster Bumblechops' gift to the city – his newly completed Moshling Sanctuary.

A huge crowd of monsters and Moshlings followed them, ready to join in with the biggest celebration Monstro City had ever seen.

As music blared from Beatboxes up and down the street, everybody high-fived or clapped along to the beat. And the crowd began to sing.

'You, you, you and me, you, you, you and me!
We're in this together united we stand.
Don't grumble, be humble and let's all join hands - hey!
You, you, you and me, you, you, you and me!
A smile's just a curve that sets everything straight,
So turn that frown upside down, don't hesitate - Smile!
Moshi Moshi mosh!
Moshi Moshi Hey!'

The Moshis reached the gates to the Sanctuary. The place was draped in bunting and decorated with balloons. The crowd of Moshlings and monsters came to a halt.

There was a sudden Poof! And, accompanied by the twanging of sitars, Jollywood gooperstar Bobbi SingSong kerfuffled into the midst of the crowd, along with a mob of his Jollywood friends, including more than one Blue Jeepers playing the sitar.

'You, you and me now!' one of Bobbi's backing singers sang.

'*We can do anything!*' the rest joined in.

'*Oh, what a kerfuffle!*' exclaimed Bobbi SingSong.

Buster Bumblechops was waiting for the friends, standing before the gates, out of his wheelchair now. Mr. Snoodle was looking particularly excited, not to mention smart in his brand-new bow-tie.

The crowd of monsters and Moshlings, including Roary Scrawl and Blinki, watched with bated breath as Katsuma stepped forward and Buster handed him a pair of scissors.

Katsuma accepted them proudly. But as he took them, he caught his reflection in the gleaming blades. He hesitated, lost in thought for a moment, and then handed the scissors to Poppet, before flashing Blinki a smile. It had taken teamwork to save the Great Moshling Egg and the whole of Moshi world from Dr. Strangeglove's nefarious plan. There wasn't just one hero in this adventure.

Poppet smiled and gave Katsuma a peck on the cheek, the orange monster blushing deeply under his fur.

Diavlo, Furi, Luvli and Zommer gathered round, putting their hands on top of Poppet's as she cut the ribbon.

A huge cheer went up from the crowd as the gates to the sanctuary swung open.

'We're in this together,' the Moshlings and monsters sang, as they all flooded through, *'we're tight, we're close knit. We never surrender, don't know when to quit!'*

A familiar chanting broke through the singing of the Moshis then as Woolly Blue Hoodoos swung down on their jungle vines. Surrounding Zommer, they bowed down before him in worship.

'Gombala, gombala, walla walla hoohaa, gombala, gombala, walla walla hoohaa!' the Hoodoos chanted, as Zommer got into the rocker vibe, throwing up gang signs and head banging as he played a brief rock riff on his guitar.

'Close but no sitar!' Bobbi declared, gesturing at one of the Blue Jeepers that then played a matching lick on its sitar.

The crowd turned its attention from the battling

musicians to Buster Bumblechops. Monstro City's renowned Moshlingologist was ready.

He was standing next to the Great Moshling Egg, massaging and stroking it – even whispering to it. The crowd of monsters and Moshlings watched in silence.

Buster grabbed the egg. Eyes closed, he began to focus mysterious, mystical Moshi energies into it. And the egg cracked.

Mr. Snoodle edged closer. Even Katsuma leaned forward, keen to witness whatever happened next.

Another fracture formed across the shell and out popped . . .

The crowd gasped.

The Moshling was another Silly Snuffler, almost identical to Mr. Snoodle in every way apart from the fact that this one had beautiful long eyelashes and a sweeping mane of rainbow hair.

Mr. Snoodle was instantly smitten and sidled up to the newly-hatched Moshling, love hearts popping in his eyes.

Buster just shrugged, looking baffled as he flicked through the ancient book in his hands, clearly flummoxed. He even turned the book upside down.

And then there it was on a page in front of him.

'I . . . I don't understand!' the Moshlingologist exclaimed in amazement. 'It's . . . Mrs. Snoodle!'

Katsuma gave a whistle of appreciation and then caught himself. 'Hey, I whistled! I whistled!'

The monsters cheered again and everyone present gave the heroes another round of applause. Roary was there in the crowd, scribbling in his notepad, while Blinki captured the moment on film. As the music played on, Buster joining in a dance with his delighted Moshlings, the residents of Monstro City ended the day with an almighty party such as Monstro City had never seen before.

CHAPTER
TWENTY-SEVEN

Later . . .

As Mr. and Mrs. Snoodle doodled off into the sunset, a certain flutterby flittered past the happy couple and away up Main Street until it left Monstro City altogether. And there it passed a pair of very bedraggled figures.

The clothes belonging to the first were ripped and torn and he had even lost his trousers. The trombone being carried by the other was badly bent out of shape.

'This is all your fault, you festering, feckless, facetious, fishlipped . . .' Strangeglove broke off as his voice grew hoarse from shouting.

The Glump at his side quickly squirted a dose of throat spray into the doctor's mouth. 'Friend?' he asked, hopefully.

Strangeglove stopped abruptly. Picking up Fishlips, he tied him up in a hanky that he then tied to the end of his cane. Slinging his glumpy sidekick over his shoulder, he set off again with a swing in his step now.

'We're in this together, although it seems odd,' Dr. Strangeglove sang.

'We're stuck with each other like peas in a pod,' Fishlips joined in. 'Urgh!'

'We're in this together,' came the distant echo of the partying Moshis, *'and that's where it ends. We know where we stand cos we stick with our friends!'*

And as Strangeglove and Fishlips headed for the horizon, the flutterby flittered on its way. It passed Poppet's garden. The pink-furred monster was planting more Moshling seeds, watched by the rest of the gang, while Katsuma entertained his new girlfriend – who was

visiting from Jollywood – tripping over the doorstep as
he brought a tray of drinks out from the house.

And the flutterby flittered on . . .

CHAPTER
TWENTY-EIGHT

Somewhere,
Deep in the Jungle . . .

The flutterby left Monstro City far behind as it flew across the sea until it reached the sweltering forests of the jungle. As the weary flutterby began to descend, the ruins of an ancient temple came into view between the vine-clung jungle trees. It was the temple where Buster Bumblechops had first discovered the Great Moshling Egg.

Flittering down to the temple steps, the flutterby alighted on a strangely familiar rock. As the insect stretched its wings, basking in the sunlight that bathed the temple clearing, the stone slowly began to sink into the ground, causing another secret entrance to open in the side of the temple.

And there, in the darkness, lay another egg – just like the one with which Dr. Strangeglove had planned to ransom the world. And beyond that lay another, and another, and another . . . Row after row of eggs, hundreds of them, all humming with ancient power . . .

The End . . .

Or is it?

MUSIC ISLAND MISSIONS

MASTERS OF THE SWOONIVERSE

T SHREWMAN

MUSIC ISLAND MISSIONS

COSMIC COUNTDOWN

T SHREWMAN